# THE
# BACKWARDS

## J. J. Hebert

MINDSTIR MEDIA

Printed in the United States of America

ISBN-13: 978-0-9993872-4-5
Library of Congress Control Number: 2017914130

Published by Mindstir Media, LLC
45 Lafayette Rd #181
North Hampton, New Hampshire 03862 | USA
1.800.767.0531 | www.mindstirmedia.com

Visit J. J. Hebert on the World Wide Web:
www.jjhebertonline.com

*This book is for Andrea.*
*She's my love and the reason I continue*
*to swing at life's opportunities.*

# CHAPTER ONE

**I STEP INTO THE ON-DECK CIRCLE,** squeezing the bat handle tight in my right hand. My heart pounds hard in my chest as I lift the bat onto my shoulder. I take a deep breath. I can hear the chants in the background, faint cries of "Let's go, Red Sox!" I try to tune out the sounds, but they overwhelm me. Sweat fills my brow. I wipe the wetness from my forehead with the heel of my batting glove.

"Let's go, Red Sox!" It grows louder.

I flash to the twelve-year-old version of myself, a young Jet Brine in the batting cages. Hundreds of swings per day, forming blisters on my hands. I think of my first home run in little league, the feeling of hitting the ball on the sweet spot, the sound of the small crowd gasping at the sound of the ball off the bat.

"Let's go, Red Sox!" The chants nearly consume me now.

I think of the high school version of myself. Home run after home run after home run. The scouts in the stands. The whispers in the crowd. The pressure. The unceasing pressure. Drafted out of high school. The *USA Today* feature articles. *SportsCenter* interviews...

"Number twelve, Jet Brine!" The sound of the PA announcer snaps me out of my trance. The memories swirl into the back of my mind. The walk-up music blares over the speakers as I leave the circle and head toward the batter's box. I cross paths with teammate Paul Frankey as he walks by me with his head hung and shoulders slouched. He drifts back to the dugout. I hear a lone fan yell out, "Swing the bat next time, Frankey!"

I step to the edge of the batter's box. I gaze out at the Green Monster, that towering wall in left field. The scoreboard reads bottom of the ninth, two outs, 3-2, their lead. This is my chance to cement my legacy—a come from behind win in the World Series. All the hard work, the endless batting practice, the thousands of swings—everything pointing to this moment...

I step into the box. My hands tremble slightly, but I work hard to hide it. I'm Jet Brine, after all. I can't tremble. I lift the bat onto my shoulder. I look beyond the pitcher at Anders on second. He's ready to soar at the crack of the bat. *We could actually win this game.* My focus moves to the pitcher. I study his face, and those dead eyes. He touches the brim of his hat and then nods. In the back of my mind I hear the talking heads from the sports talk shows, the ones I'd never admit listening to.

"Brine could be the x-factor for the Series..."

"He needs to work on his pitch selection..."

I shake off the thoughts. The pitcher comes to a set. The crowd silences. This is it. The windup and the high leg kick... I search for the ball. My hands tighten over the handle. I see the ball fly out of his hand. The ball hisses through the air. I see the seams rolling toward me. I take a cut, the biggest cut of my life. The ball smacks the glove behind me, producing a loud *pop*.

Strike one.

The crowd gasps in unison.

The pitcher smirks. I contemplate those lifeless eyes once again. He thinks he owns me. I look past him at Anders. He takes a large lead. The sweat spreads over my brow once more. I wipe it off with a batting glove as before.

Here it comes, *the* moment of my life. The wind-up and high leg kick. The release and the sound of the ball cutting through the air. The ball whizzes by at waist height. I can't lift the bat off my shoulder for whatever reason.

*"Strike!"* The ump cranks his right arm.

The gasps float through the air.

I think of Janice, my beautiful wife in the crowd somewhere behind me. I'm failing the fans as I've failed her. I can't help but recall our fight from last night. The shouts load my mind and nearly devour me. I see her saddened face in my mind's eye, her tired and disappointed eyes. I'm the villain. I'm always the villain.

*Must. Focus. Now.* I snap out of it.

I'm down to my last chance here. I feel the overwhelming burden of the millions of fans watching in the world. I can picture them sitting around their TVs. I imagine the broadcasters casting their doubts. The thought nearly smothers me. I can almost literally feel the weight on my shoulders. They're heavier now, weighed down by the fear. One more strike and it's over. I can be the hero or the villain—it's up to me.

I stand in the box and ready myself. The chants resume. "Come on, Jet Brine!" Chills shoot down my spine. I've waited for this moment my entire life. The pitcher goes through his motions and everything plays out in slow motion. The ball tumbles toward me and I swear I can see every red stitch. I go to swing—and I really want to—but I can't. I just can't. The ball passes me by and the ump rings me up—a *"Strike three"* uttered somewhere in the distance, practically in some other world. It's the old backwards K, the strikeout looking. This time it just happened to be in Game 7 of the freakin' World Series.

I hang my head and I want to crumble to the ground. The weight presses down on me, like an elephant sitting on my shoulders. Boos flow through the air. Fans are no longer fans. They scream and shout as they would at an enemy...

# CHAPTER TWO

**I SLAM THE ALARM CLOCK** with my fist but the beeping continues mercilessly. I peek at the clock that reads **6:30**. I catch a glimpse of my face in the mirror on the wall behind the clock, probably the first time I've seen myself in weeks, and it's like I'm looking at a stranger. It feels like yesterday I was waking up to put on my uniform. Those days are long gone and this lonely old man, with peppered gray hair and weary eyes, is all that remains of the mighty Jet Brine.

I drag myself out of bed. I don't bother shaving or showering. I grab my duffle bag by the door, throw on a jacket and leave my one-bedroom hole of an apartment. It's January in New England. That means shoveling, lots of shoveling, and clearing off my rusted-out car. After what feels like hours, I'm finally able to drive out of the parking lot, and after a couple of minutes, onto I-95.

I look in my rearview mirror at the duffle bag in the backseat. I don't know why I'm doing this. I should have stayed home. Do I really need the money *this* badly? Janice's blanched face emerges in my mind—the version of my wife in the hospital bed, tubes jammed up her nose, forearm wrapped in gauze, and machines humming around her. Our tumultuous relationship haunts me. All the fighting, counseling, shutting her out as I put nearly my entire focus on my baseball dream and the money—*oh God, the money*—none of that mattered when I saw her on the bed that day. It was too late for us by that point.

That tattered duffle bag in the backseat is all that's left of my big baseball career and the fortune. Everything I worked so hard for sits in a single duffle bag. That's right. I look up at the road and see the giant green exit sign for Boston. I slowly turn onto the exit.

I arrive at the convention center a few minutes later. I pass by whispering men and women as I approach the entrance with my bag in hand. "Is that Jet Brine?" The whispers sound the same these days.

A half-hour later and my table is nearly set up with the merchandise. I remove the last item from my bag and place it on the table. It's a bobblehead doll, the 2024 edition of Jet Brine, signed by yours truly. Maybe I'll get a hundred bucks for it. I look down my long table filled with Jet Brine collectibles. I organize my 8x10 photos into a neat stack and place the black Sharpie next to the photos. The front doors open in the distance and the sound of footsteps and chattering pack the room.

I look over at the table to my right and then to my left. White-haired ex-ball players man those tables, too. Some hold canes and some hold thirty or forty extra pounds on their frames these days. We're here for one reason, and it's not the glory: We need the money. Many of us fell into money very early in life, before we knew how to handle it responsibly. I honestly feel a bit like a cheap prostitute, selling myself for a few dollars, but I need this money to survive.

I sit on my stool and wait. I wait for a solid twenty minutes or so before a kid and his father approach me.

"Tim, this is Jet Brine." The dad points to me like I'm an animal at a zoo. "He was big when I was growing up."

I'm not sure how to react, so I throw on my default phony smile, the one I used during my baseball interview days. I hold out my hand and shake theirs. The father points to a small stack of baseball cards on the corner of the table.

"Oh, wow," says the dad, "I remember those..." The son rolls his eyes.

I hand the cards to the father. "Yeah, those are classics," I say.

He pulls one from the pile and holds it up. The price tag reads $25. "How much for this one?" he asks.

I want to be the one rolling my eyes now, but I force a smile once again. "$25," I say calmly. I realize he wants to haggle, but I'm not having it.

The man inspects my face, searching for weakness. "How about $20?" he asks.

I politely decline the offer.

The man returns the card back to the heap and drops the stack onto the table. A red flush creeps up his face. "That's all right. He's the guy who blew the Series anyways," he mutters.

Maybe a few years ago this would have taken me aback, but it's commonplace today. He struts away before I can utter another word.

Hours pass. I deal with maybe a dozen people directly. I sell about one-hundred-fifty-dollars' worth of collectibles and make eye contact with the occasional glaring passerby. Despite achieving a career batting average of .301 and generating over 2,000 hits, some people just can't get over my backwards K in the World Series. It was my defining moment for some, apparently. Sometimes I believe that myself.

I leave the facility and drive away. After paying the $50 fee for the table, I have one hundred dollars in my pocket and a duffle bag in the backseat nearly filled to the zipper. These conventions were once big, money-making events, but those times have passed. I guess people would rather be doing other things these days.

I drive by a casino. My fingers tingle on the steering wheel. I'm tempted to make a pit stop and throw my hundred-dollar bill at the slot machines, but I will myself to keep driving this time. My stomach roars at me; I need to use the money to eat.

I stop at a run-down fifties diner off the interstate. The waitress approaches the table. Her eyes protrude from her skull. "You're... you're," she stammers. I nod and give a half-smile. Her entire face lights up. I order pancakes and she strides away.

I ponder the future, alone in a dirty booth in the middle of nowhere. I picture myself as an old man with a cane, hawking my collectibles. I gasp at the thought.

I resolve to get a job, a real, honorable job that pays consistently.

———————

Sitting in the lobby, I eyeball my black Timex watch where my Rolex once sat. It's four o'clock sharp. I look to the far wall above the busy secretary as she slaps her fingers on the keyboard. The company's logo adorns the wall. Behind me, through a door apparently leading to the shop, muffled power tools hum and buzz. I twist around and peek through one of the door windows to see the busy shop. Men and women, mostly middle-aged, effortlessly put their tools to use on long, unfinished planks of wood.

"Mr. Brine." The voice yanks my attention away from the door.

I stand up abruptly, adjust my tie and then extend an open hand.

The rotund, spectacled woman shakes my hand and introduces herself as Maggy Simons, head of Human Resources. She guides me into a small glass-encased room near the lobby. I sit in one of the only two seats in the room. She sits on the opposite end of the desk and pulls out a folder and a pen. She starts tapping on the desk with her pen. She has lines in her face and worn-out eyes. I notice a ketchup stain on her blouse. It's a light stain, like she tried in vain to remove it with a wet cloth.

"Now, Mr. Brine, it's a pleasure to have you here today," she says. She looks at me squarely in the eyes. "I enjoyed our phone interview the other day and felt compelled to meet you in person... I see you have limited work experience, but I'm always willing to give those with life experience a shot, as long as they're open-minded and willing to learn."

"I'm very open-minded and a fast learner."

Her mouth curves into a smile. "That's good to hear." She pushes her glasses up the ridge of her nose. "Given your experience in Major League Baseball as a team captain as well as your charitable work throughout years, I'm confident that you're a man of integrity and would fit well here personality-wise and values-wise."

"I really appreciate that."

"My only concern, and I touched on this with you previously, is the gap in your resumé. I see you held some part-time jobs during your youth, but I don't see a work history post-baseball. Care to elaborate?"

I gather my thoughts. "Well, admittedly, this would be a new type of gig for me." Nervously, I adjust my tie once more. "Baseball took care of my financial needs for many years, but those checks stopped coming long ago, and I'm ready for a new phase in my life, so I figured it was time."

She gives a double-nod. "So, you need the money," she says, a statement, not a question.

"Basically."

"At least you're honest. I wouldn't expect anything less from you." She jots down some notes. I squint at her notepad, attempting to decipher her handwriting from across the table. I can't make out her scrawls.

"Of course, money would be nice, but I'm also looking for new experiences," I say. I don't want to be perceived only as a desperate, money-hungry man.

She sets down her pen, puts the paper in the folder and closes it. We sit in silence. A couple men in suits scurry by our room. They laugh as they dash down the hallway.

"I'll be honest, Mr. Brine," she says. "I like you. I've liked you since our initial conversation, but I wanted an opportunity to size you up..."

I stare at her, trying to think of an appropriate response.

She continues, "I'll give you a shot. We'll start you out in data entry and evaluate you from there."

Never in a million years would I have thought I'd be so happy to hear those words. But all I can think of is my bank account. My last bank statement haunts me: $525.36 AVAILABLE BALANCE. I won't be able to make rent without this job.

I thank her for the opportunity and tell her I won't let her down. I know it's a clichéd thing to say, but I know I won't let her down. I don't have a choice. I need to eat, to have a roof over my head, to survive...

# CHAPTER THREE

**MY ALARM BLARES**. My eyes flutter open, and stare at the water-stained ceiling. I don't have the energy to slam the clock today. I groan as I get out of the creaking bed. I ready myself for my first day of work—a real job. I head to work wearing my second-best suit and tie. My other suit, my only other suit, is at the cheapest cleaners in town. Plus, I last wore it at the interview with Maggy, and I don't want them to think I only own one suit like some sort of hobo. Although, I hardly think a hobo owns any suits. *Oh well.*

I park in a lined spot far away from the entrance. My heart bangs hard against my chest. I have trouble swallowing. My hands tremble slightly. My breath rushes in and out. I close my eyes. I envision a smiling Janice, not the hospital version but instead the gardening version, the Janny who used to smile over the flowers in her garden. She wears one of her straw hats. She holds a gardening tool and looks back at me, filling me with warmth...

I puff out a breath, steadying myself. I exit the car. I advance across the large parking lot, calculating each step to keep my balance. I stop at the box-like brick building. I'm an alien and that's an uncharted planet. I take another labored breath. I open the front door, enter the lobby, my shoes scuffing the entryway rug. I look up, my face warming. The same secretary as before welcomes me with a smile—not a Janny-caliber smile but a smile nonetheless. The secretary pages the manager, Holly.

Holly bursts through a nearby door a few moments later, her hair disheveled.

She brings me to her office in a hurry. She slides a dog-eared company handbook across her teakwood desk. It's mostly a rulebook composed of the company policies. "Make sure you study that," she says hastily. I smile at her often and try to exude positive energy. My hands vibrate on the armrests.

I keep trying to think of Janice's smile, her bright, glowing smile...

Holly shows me around the sales office. "We have to make this quick," she says with force. "I have a meeting in ten minutes." She points to my cubicle consisting of my very own food-stained desk and outdated computer. *I need to start somewhere, I guess.*

"Have a seat and I'll send someone your way in a moment to start your training." Holly dashes off.

Co-workers sit in their own cubicles on either side of me and throughout the sales office. Phones ring. Metal drawers rattle open and crash closed. Voices rise and fall. Awaiting the ominous training, I force air from my lungs, my clammy hand tapping against a bouncing knee.

---

During the first few days, I mostly learn to re-enter purchase orders into our software, Oracle.

I'm not the most proficient person with computers, so the learning curve is steep, and I'm constantly unsure of myself and my skills. I ask a lot of questions and see a few eyes roll and heads shake.

Some of the older workers in the office obviously want nothing to do with me. They avoid eye contact for the most part. They dodge my attempts at conversations; they're always "too busy" for me.

We get a half-hour lunch break each day. I usually eat my lunch in the car, isolated as in life, but today I'm determined to change gears, to try something new. I enter the lunch room with my brown bag. The room is cold and contains a small pantry kitchen with a refrigerator, microwave, and sink. Identical tables line the floor. One table is taken by three men playing a card game. A man with thick glasses and a scruffy, long gray beard sits at another table. He looks around the room with heavy eyelids. Then I notice a beaming woman sitting alone at one of the tables, a sandwich in hand, her smile eerily familiar. *Just like Janice used to smile...* I approach the table and ask to join her, holding up my bag. She gives me another smile and nod. Warmth shoots through my veins.

She introduces herself as Linda, and we shake hands. She wears her dark hair in a bun. A black dress envelops her slender body. "So how long have you been working here?" she inquires. She sounds genuinely interested. Her blue eyes pierce me.

I haven't been this nervous since my first date with Janny many years ago. I feel the sweat on my forehead. I no longer have a batting glove to wipe it clean. "Just long enough to notice you're one of the only friendly faces in the office," I quip.

She chuckles. "Corporate America does that to some." She takes a bite of her sandwich, then inquisitively, "You work in sales, right?"

I nod. "The department, yeah, but right now I'm just entering orders. Getting the hang of it."

She smiles again. "I worked in sales at one point... back in the day. Count yourself lucky that you're just entering orders. Sales is no picnic."

"No?"

She puts down the sandwich, starts tickling her hair. "It's not for the faint-hearted. It's very stressful." She pauses. "But you're no stranger to stress, are you?"

I cock my head. "How so?"

"I know who you are." She gives a slight grin.

I incline my head again. "Oh?"

Her eyes begin to glimmer. I swear they flicker. "I used to watch you..."

I'm taken aback by her statement. She seems to notice; her eyes light up. *Has she been stalking me? A beautiful woman stalking me?*

"You were my father's favorite ballplayer," she clarifies.

I release an exaggerated sigh of relief.

She laughs. "I'm not crazy or anything. Promise."

"I appreciate that." I catch a whiff of her perfume, a floral scent. "So, then, I guess you know everything about me?" I ask with a facetious tone.

"Well, not *everything*, I'm sure."

I can't tell if that has a veiled sexual connotation.

Silence overcomes the table. We go on eating for a couple moments, and I finally muster another sentence: "So which department do you work in now?"

She pulls a business card from her pocket and slides it across the table. It reads **VP OF OPERATIONS**. I chuckle inside. *Of course.*

Her eyebrows dance. "Yeah, I'm not a stranger to stress, either, as you can see." She points toward the card.

"I guess not."

We chat for another few minutes. She tells me more about her father. Cancer stole him away two years ago. He loved the Sox, watched nearly every game. Impressive seeing as how each season consists of least 162 games not including playoffs.

"He was a bit of a fanatic," she recalls in a soft voice. "He had boxes and boxes of baseball cards. Signed bats and balls as well."

I think of my time at the conventions peddling my items. "Anything in there of mine?" I ask.

"Probably." She presses her lips together. "He had everything." She looks down at the table, her eyes suddenly somber. "Well, everything... except for his health..." She pauses and then taps on her gold watch, and looks back up at me. "I'd better get going. It was great speaking with you, Mr. Brine."

I beam. "You too, Linda. I'll see you around."

———

Days pass. The outfits change, but everything at work remains virtually the same. I sit at my desk, eyeballing orders with worn-out eyes, hands slapping the keys day after day. I'm like a trained monkey.

I look for Linda daily but don't spot her in the cafeteria or anywhere. I daydream about her in between orders. I feel kind of guilty about my daydreams, almost like I'm cheating on Janice. I know that's not the case, but I can't help but feel it.

One of my cubicle neighbors, Peggy, loves to play country music. She also owns a terrible high-pitched squeal of a voice, like fingernails on a chalkboard. She yaps on her phone nearly all day. At times, I need to leave my cubicle to escape her sound.

My other cubicle neighbor, Fred, insists on eating at his desk. It wouldn't be so bad if his favorite food wasn't always egg-related. Egg salad sandwiches, hard-boiled eggs. Eggs, eggs, and more eggs.

I look up all too often at the wall clock hanging over my cubicle. Its hands click in slow motion over its face. Five o'clock can never come quickly enough.

"Jet..." A voice from behind me catches my attention.

I spin around in my chair. My manager greets me with a smile. Holly invites me to her office. I can't tell by her tone if she wants to discuss something positive or negative. I stand up and pass Peggy's country-music-blaring cubicle and move through the room to Holly's office.

"Have a seat," she says, motioning to the chair in front of her desk. She joins me at her desk and starts ruffling through some papers.

"I'll cut right to the chase, Jet. I've heard some complaints."

I swallow hard. "Complaints?"

"Yes," she says sternly. I haven't seen this side of her before. She continues, "You seem to be catching on quickly around here, but your overall pace needs some work."

I try not to appear defensive. I really don't know how to react or what to say, so I pause. She doesn't seem to enjoy long gaps in conversation; she interjects, "Most of our data entry folks are able to enter at least one hundred orders per day but you're stuck around the fifty-order mark."

A mix of shame and fear rattle my insides. "I'm very sorry. I'll try to move at a faster pace from now on."

"I'd appreciate the added effort." Her attention turns to her computer screen. "I'll continue to monitor the situation going forward." She speaks absently, her eyes moving side to side over the computer screen, reading something.

I wait for her attention to revert to me, but her eyes remain glued to the monitor. She stabs a finger toward the door. "That'll be all for now, Jet."

———

Days blend together.

I try to pick up the pace. I reach one hundred orders in a day for the first time. No one seems to notice or care. I can't say I feel any fulfillment from meeting the goal, either. I'm just entering orders after all, but at least I'll get to keep my job, pay the rent and continue eating for now.

I finally bump into Linda in the cafeteria. We lock eyes and sit at the same table as before. She reaches into her pocket and pulls out a card. I wonder why she's handing me another business card. I grab for the card and realize it's a base-ball card of myself.

"Pulled that from one of my dad's boxes," she says. "He had two or three of them."

I inspect the card—the glossy front and back and the sharp corners. It's in mint condition.

"So, will you sign it?" She hands me a pen. She obviously came prepared.

"Of course." I sign the card and hand it back to her.

"Dad will love this," she says.

I wonder about her statement. *How will her dad enjoy this? Hasn't he passed?* I simply nod and smile.

"So... I've been thinking..." she says, piquing my interest. "Perhaps we could get a bite to eat outside of work at some point."

*Is she really asking me out?* "That sounds great," I blurt. She giggles. Then I think that maybe I should have dialed back the enthusiasm. I don't want to sound too eager.

We set up a dinner meeting or date. I'm not sure if it's a date or a friendly meeting.

Janice's face materializes in my mind. I wonder if she'd be okay with this. I still feel like a cheating jerk, but I try to convince myself otherwise. *She'd want me to be happy,* I reassure myself often. And she would. She was always a people-pleaser, always wanted everyone to be happy. That was Janny.

# CHAPTER FOUR

SATURDAY ARRIVES. I leave my apartment and trudge through the snow to the shared mailbox for the apartment building. Like the days before this, the apartment manager has sorted the mail by name. I find an envelope without a return address and it's clearly addressed to Jet Brine. I open the letter where I stand. I see my cold breath wafting over the letter as I read it.

Dear Jet,

I know you don't do much with email nowadays so I thought I'd just shoot you this letter. I hope it finds you well. We have a great thing going out here. We're about to draft Pinkins in the 1st round. He reminds me a lot of you, actually. Great swing and fast as a horse. Really good kid, too.

*Anyway, the offer is still on the table. I'd love for you to come out here and give it a shot. You've always had the eye. I'm sure it could seamlessly translate to scouting. Give me a call sometime.*

Paul Frankey, my teammate from years ago. I see his cell phone number at the bottom of the page near his name. I fold up the letter and tuck it in my pants pocket. He's sent me three or four of these types of letters throughout the years. I've never replied. Not once. I just can't do it for whatever reason. Maybe because the thought of being involved in baseball again is too painful, too raw. *Conventions are one thing but actually being near a baseball field?*

I visualize myself as a scout, wearing the old cap and windbreaker jacket, sitting behind home plate with a radar gun pointed at the field. I imagine everyone staring at me, the old, washed-up Jet Brine, the one who blew the World Series.

I cringe.

I stop at a gas station, and exit the car. The bitter, cold wind blows across my face, stinging it. I shiver as I fill up the car. I swipe my debit card through the reader. **CARD READING ERROR** flashes on the screen. I briefly wonder if my card has insufficient funds, but I recall that I got paid last week. I go inside the store. I hand the card to the cashier and state the number of the pump.

The middle-aged cashier looks at me with wide eyes. "You're..."

"Yeah..."

He rings me up, hands me the receipt. He pulls out his cell. "Do you mind if we get a picture? Tom won't believe this!"

I look at my watch. I need to be at Linda's in ten minutes. I don't want to be late for our—

"It will be quick, I promise," the cashier says, almost as if reading my mind.

I nod and agree to it. He lurches from behind the counter and quickly snaps a selfie with me. He looks at the screen and smiles. "Tom will love this. You're like his hero."

I grin. It's nice to still have a few fans remaining.

"Yeah, you're the reason his team won that season..." The cashier clarifies.

My heart sinks. I hear the boos in some far-away place. I want to yell at this guy, to tell him how I feel about this interaction, how incredibly tacky this whole situation is, but I need to meet with Linda. I need to go. *Now*. I dash out of the store and jump into my car.

I reach into a pocket, fish around for the keys, and feel Paul Frankey's letter. I remove the keys and the letter, one in each hand. I crumple the letter up into a ball with one hand. I toss it over a shoulder into the backseat, my veins pulsing.

I arrive at Linda's barely on time. I pull up to the white brick home and goggle at the sheer opulence. Trees flank the driveway. Columns line the entrance and what looks to be a four-car garage sits off to the right of the entrance. I park my rust-box in front of the garage and walk to the door. I knock a couple times. I half expect a butler to answer the door. She opens the door instead, her long red dress flowing, and all I can think is *Lady in Red.*

"Come on in," she says, shivering from the wind whipping through the open door. "You must be freezing."

I step through. She shuts the door behind me. We both stand in her entryway.

"Can I take your coat?"

"Yes, thank you." I remove my coat and hand it to her. My hand grazes hers during the hand off, sending a wave of warmth through my body. She hangs the coat on a wall hook, turns back around and our eyes meet. Her pupils expand. An invisible magnet draws me closer to her. I want to hold her, press her body against mine. I want to bury myself in her warmth.

She interrupts the silence, "I hope you don't mind. I'll be back down in a minute." She darts off into a side room. Guilt stabs at me. I wonder if I've done something to offend her.

I step into the living room. I look up at the crystal chandelier. I sit on her loveseat. I once owned a house like this—several times the size, before Janice's untimely death. I think of my apartment now and how Linda and I live at opposite ends of the spectrum, but she doesn't seem to know or care.

I trace the walls with my gaze and land on a framed picture of her and a white-haired man. *He must be her father.* I continue scanning the room. My focus stops at the fireplace, more specifically the mantel. I squint from across the room. *Is that what I think it is?* I drift over to the mantel. I stare at the urn, her father's urn. I blink hard. My signed baseball card is propped up to the right of the urn.

I hear footsteps behind me, and I turn around.

"I told you he'd enjoy it," she says. She points toward the urn and the card. A tear rolls down her cheek like rain on a dusty pane. "I'm sorry..." She lets out a wounded chuckle, her eyelids puffy.

I suck back tears. I try sniffing discretely. I shake my head. "You don't need to apologize."

She forces air from her lungs. She abruptly changes the subject: "So how do I look?"

I chuckle nervously. "You look amazing..."

*Lady in Red.*

# CHAPTER FIVE

**LINDA AND I SIT IN A COFFEE SHOP** a week before Christmas. I often wonder why she'd want to hang around someone like me. And she's my superior at work, so we're sometimes unsure how to act around one another at work. But here, away from the daily grind, we can be ourselves.

"So where do you see this going?" she asks out of the blue. She obviously realizes the pointedness of her question because she grins.

"You mean *this?*" I point to her and then to myself.

She nods.

"I see it going wherever it decides to go." I speak in a riddle.

"I'm not ESPN, Jet." She takes a sip of her coffee. "You can be candid with me."

"I think we definitely have something here," I say. "Something really good." I pause. "I'm hopeful."

"Good," she says. "We're not getting any younger, you know." She nods at the table across from us.

I look to the table. The young couple reminds me of Janice and me decades ago. The couple holds hands and smiles wide. They don't look a day older than twenty. I bring my attention back to Linda. "Wouldn't it be nice to be twenty again?" I ask.

"But then I wouldn't be here with you," she says.

"Good point." I bite into my dry muffin.

She studies me closely. "I try to live a life without regrets."

I don't know how to respond. *My life is full of regrets.* I wish I had been a better, more attentive husband. I wish I had swung at that fateful pitch. I wish I had saved my money, stayed away from the horrors of gambling. *I wish Jay—*

"What are your regrets?" she finally asks.

I knew this was coming but I freeze.

She puts a hand on mine. "You can confide in me..."

"You're probably aware of at least one of them," I say.

"That wasn't your fault. It was a borderline strike." She seemingly reads my mind.

I think of all the times throughout the years that I've replayed the video clip. It wasn't a borderline strike; it was a strike nearly right down the middle. She's trying to make me feel better. She's like Janice, the people-pleaser.

"You were a great ballplayer," Linda reminisces. "My dad would vouch for that." She sips on her coffee. "You can't let your whole life be defined by one strikeout, Jet. You're much more than one at bat."

———

I stand from my frayed couch, and head to the kitchen. My stomach rumbles. I open the fridge, and see the lone slab of meat on a plate. I shake my head. *Living high off the hog.* I can still hear

Linda's words from the other night, about not allowing one at bat to define me, but that's easier said than done.

I grab the meat and throw it on the grill. The smell instantly transports me back in time. I see a dark-haired Jet grilling a steak in a palatial home, a little boy named Jay running around barefoot and in a diaper, yelling, "Daddy, Daddy, Daddy..." My son. He just wants my attention but I withhold it from him. I have other things to think about, other worries in the world: My baseball career, my money, my gambling. Jay circles me and he can't stop saying my name. I'm his daddy, his one and only daddy. But I'm not. I'm barely his father. I've heard the saying that anyone can be a father, but not everyone is a daddy. That's spot-on. I barely see him. Janice tells me of his cute mannerisms, how much alike we are, but I look past them, past him, and I never see any of it...

Searing pain in my hand brings me back to the present. I slam the spatula on the counter, turn off the stove and start crying. My lower lip quivers. I must have accidentally touched the pan, but I'm not crying because of that. I pull out my wallet and remove a picture of Jay. He's much older in the photo, a teenager. He's smiling wide. He has his mother's smile. A tear drips onto the photo. I wipe the wetness from his face.

Linda was right—that one at bat didn't define me. It was this one, this one at bat called fatherhood. I struck out looking every time. Every. Single. Time. To this day, he resides merely in my pocket, out of sight and out of mind.

Jay was my first life-changing backwards K.

———

I'm dreaming. It's one of those dreams in which I know I'm dreaming. I see Janice. She marches over to me. I realize we're standing in the garden, *Janny's* garden. She's wearing her customary straw hat, smiling. I reach out to her, to touch her hand, to touch her somewhere, anywhere, to see if she's real. But I know she isn't.

She finally reaches out and takes my hand into hers. I can feel her hand, its smoothness and warmth, and I start to lose it. She's real. This isn't a dream. This can't be a dream. This is too real. I remember how my wife feels.

She says softly, "I'm okay."

I'm simultaneously relieved and confused. "Is this heaven?" I ask.

"This is wherever you need it to be." She tightens her grip.

"Wherever I need it to be?"

"I want you to see that I'm happy. I want you to be happy," she says.

"But..."

She looks directly into my eyes. "I want you to be happy," she repeats.

Her face, her body, they start to swirl and mix together, and then everything fades to black.

———————

Linda grabs my hand. "Come on!" We trek to the fountain. Families surround us here in the mall. Christmas elevator music plays softly in the background. We step to the fountain pool in the near-center of the mall. We sit on the edge of the pool adorned with Christmas decorations, the fountain trickling behind us. I rest my hand on her knee.

"We have to talk," she says.

My heart drops. I remove my hand from her leg. "About what?" I ask. I partially don't want to know. I contemplate standing up and walking away. At least then she wouldn't be able to give any bad news.

"I feel that our relationship is moving very quickly," she continues.

"I've really enjoyed our time together. I hope—"

"Just listen for a moment," she interrupts.

"Okay..."

She restarts: "I feel that our relationship is moving very quickly... and I'm glad that it is."

I heave a sigh. "I feel the same way."

"What I'm really getting around to," she says, "what I really want to ask you is, will you celebrate Christmas with me this year?" She recognizes my relief. "This is a big deal for me, inviting you to meet my family..."

"Of course, I'll go." I place my hand back onto her knee.

She leans in and kisses me. Her breath tastes like spearmint. I feel as if I'm floating. She looks down at my hand and smiles. We sit in silence, listening to the trickling waters and festive music.

I think of Janice, my surreal dream. Her face swims into view. I think, *Today I'm happy.* Janice beams in my mind and my body overfills with warmth.

# CHAPTER SIX

A FOUR-YEAR-OLD JAY, in his blue footed pajamas, circles the Christmas tree, arms waving in excitement. "Presents!" he squeals.

Janice grabs him up and hugs him. She kisses his cheeks. "Mommy..." He giggles and then looks over to me sitting on the couch, hinting for me to join them. I stand from the couch and awkwardly join the hugging fest. I'm like a foreigner trying to learn some bizarre ritual.

I grab a nearby present from under the imposing tree, no doubt a gift that Janice picked out. I hand it to Jay. Jay tears apart the wrapping paper, absolutely obliterating it. He pulls out a video game. The cover depicts some colorful little dog-like creatures, and he yells their names one-by-one. I know I'm *supposed* to know who they are; he's said the names before, but

I'm never truly listening. I fake a smile. I feel like a failure, an absent father, never truly a dad.

Janice seizes another wrapped gift, a box, and hands it to him. It's one of those recordable, talking frames. Jay looks puzzled.

Janice turns her gaze to me. "You can record a message for him," she says. "This way he can hear your voice every day."

I know she means well, but her words stab at my chest. He tosses the frame to the side and selects his own present this time. He shakes it and it rattles. He fiercely removes the wrapping and lifts some encased baseball cards from the box. He studies the cards intently. He holds a card up to my eye level and my face stares back at me; it's my Topps rookie card. Jay giggles again and sorts through the other cards.

I eye my wristwatch and stand. "Well, it's time to hit the road."

Janice and Jay drop their shoulders in near-unison. They look back at me.

"But I thought we'd have you here for once..." she says desperately.

"I know, but I need to get some more swings in today in the cage. It's gonna be a big season."

She shakes her head with disapproval. "Spring training isn't until February... I thought we already discussed this."

"*Janice*," I say sternly, upset that she's making a scene in front of Jay. I can see Jay in the corner of my eye watching us.

"Don't *Janice* me... You'd rather spend your afternoon, Christmas afternoon, in the cages than with your family?" Her voice quivers. Her face turns crimson.

"You knew what you were getting into when you married me," I say, wagging my finger at her. "You know how important my career is."

She huffs. "If I only knew, Jet. If I only knew..." Her jaw clenches.

A few minutes later I'm standing in the indoor batting cages. I throw on a helmet and my batting gloves. A couple of my teammates, Harris and Welton, swing away in the neighboring cages.

I step into my cage, bat in hand, and get into a proper stance. The ball comes screaming at me. I swing and rip it back at the machine. Another pitch hisses toward me and I hit it squarely. The crash of the bat echoes throughout the area.

Repeatedly, the pitches come in and leave with a loud crack of the bat. I take hundreds of cuts until I realize that I'm the only one remaining in the room. I step out of the cage and take a seat on the adjacent bench. I sit here, leaning forward with elbows on my knees, alone in the silence.

*Merry Christmas*, I think to myself.

———

I sit on the couch in Linda's living room. Christmas tunes and the smell of freshly baked cookies waft through the air. The grand Christmas tree stands in the corner of the room and the star at the top tickles the ceiling. Linda sits on the floor with her nephew, sister, and brother-in-law. Nephew Erick shakes a few presents and throws out guesses of their contents. Everyone in the room chuckles. I can't help but think of Jay, years before.

Linda's mother, Ruth, sits in a recliner to my left. Her cane rests on the side of the chair. "So, Linny was telling me that you recently landed a job at her company."

I fidget on my cushion. I tell her about my data entry position, how it's mostly menial work at the moment, but it pays the bills. "Although it did introduce me to your daughter." I plaster a smile on my face.

She chuckles. "Sounds like it's been well worth it, then," she quips.

"For sure."

Ruth nods in the direction of the mantle. "It's a nice thing you did for us," she says. "Pops always did love you." She looks to my signed baseball card, then to Linda, then back to me. "You make her happy, you know," she whispers. She sizes me up and down. "I can tell you're a good boy."

I grin and thank her for the compliment.

"We've never had an athlete in our family," she says.

I feel my eyes widen at that last statement. *Our family...*

The growing giggling of Nephew Erick pulls my attention away from Ruth and to the tree area. His mother kisses him on the cheeks in between opening presents. Linda laughs.

The past comes roaring back in my mind. Nephew Erick transforms into Jay and my heart burns so much that I swear it's bleeding. I look to Linda; she plays the role of Janice. She starts kissing him on the cheeks and hugging him. The room shifts and bends until I find myself sitting in my own living room from the past.

My eyes well with tears. I want to reach out and touch them. I want to feel their skin to know they're real. I want a do-over. This time I'd jump up from the couch and join their hugging and kissing without any awkwardness at all. I'd stay for all the presents. I'd just stay—

A voice calling my name catches me off guard. Linda leans over me on the couch. "Are you okay?" she whispers. Her mother looks on from the side.

I wipe the tears away with my hand. "Not really…"

"What happened?"

I can't articulate it here, not now. I fear that I might completely break down in front of everyone here. I stand abruptly, panicking. "I have to go."

She falters backward. "*Go?* Go where? Are you all right?"

The people in the room fall silent. The music remains as the lone sound.

Then I hear Ruth un-recline her chair. She leans in more closely, hovering. She has the cane in her hand now. Linda moves to the side to block off her mother's view.

"I'm sorry, I just have to go. I'm a mess…"

After seeing a blur of moving bodies and hearing sounds of distorted, puzzled voices, I get in my car and drive away from Linda's party. Tears break free and stream down my face. I turn the dial on the radio. Every station features

Christmas music, haunting me. I turn off the radio. Light snow falls onto my windshield as I move further away from Linda's. My heart continues to burn. It's scorched as if on fire, and I don't know how to extinguish it.

I just keep driving and driving. I want to drive forever, far away from this place, away from my memories, but the car can't go fast enough. I look to the passenger's seat at one point and think I see Janice sitting there. I look in my rearview mirror and see toddler Jay in his car seat, returning the stare. Tears fall like rain on my lap.

Then I see the sign, those blinking lights, my savior: **CASINO**. I take the turn and pull into the lit parking lot. I grab my wallet. I open it to find three twenty-dollar bills. I shut the wallet. I sit in the lot and wipe away these tears. My thoughts transition to the slots. I can hear the jackpot bells in my mind. My heart cools.

I depart the car on this cold Christmas evening and skulk to the casino's entrance, alone in the silence.

# CHAPTER SEVEN

**THE EARLY-MORNING SUN BLINDS ME** as I amble to my snow-covered car. I brush off my car and leave the casino parking lot. I take my cell phone out of my pocket, glance down to discover it's off, that the battery has been drained. I plug the cell into my car charger as I drive down a snow-dusted Main Street.

My stomach grumbles. I keep an eye out for a restaurant, any restaurant open at six a.m. I spot a diner ten minutes later and pull in. Inside, a worn-out hostess greets me with a forged smile and tired voice. "Table for one... right this way..."

I follow her to a table. I sit down and set my bulging wallet and cell on the table to my right. I thumb through the menu. Soft Christmas music plays somewhere overhead. I roll my eyes. I end up ordering eggs benedict.

The food arrives and I catch a whiff. My taste buds ache. I inhale the meal. The waitress drops off the bill and I open my wallet. I flip through several one-hundred-dollar bills before I get to a group of twenties. I drop a twenty on the table and turn on my recently somewhat-charged cell. The voicemail notification window pops up on the screen and flashes **3 MESSAGES.** I tap the graphic and the first message starts playing automatically.

"Jet, I don't know what happened or why you had to leave but please call me. Okay? Please call me right back. I'll be up for another hour or so." Linda's voice breaks. "Call me any time of the night, all right? I just want to hear from you."

The second message plays and I quickly recognize her voice. My shoulders slump. "I can't sleep," she says. "It's like three and I can't sleep. We were all worried about you. Please call me back."

My eyes squeeze shut. The third message plays: "I'm starting to think the worst, Jet. I really need to hear from you this morning. Please call me."

I decide to call her. She doesn't pick up. I call again. Nothing.

Back in the car, my phone rings. I press the green button. She explains how relieved she is to hear from me. "I'm just glad you're alive," she says. She asks to get together later today. I hesitantly accept her invitation.

We meet at the same coffee shop as before and sit at our usual table. One other person sits in a far-off corner sipping his coffee from a tin mug. I skip the coffee this time and opt for a blueberry scone. I pick at the pastry as she stirs the sugar into her coffee.

She looks up at me, sets her spoon down. "My mom was really concerned," she says. "Everyone was really concerned, including me."

"I'm sorry about that," I say dryly. I bite into the scone.

"That's *it?*" Her eyes flash with anger. "This is kind of a big deal, you know..." I can hear the disappointment in her voice.

"I just had to go." I take a break from chewing.

"I invited you to meet my family. Christmas was secondary. I've been talking you up around the clock, and then you flaked out. I don't know what to tell them now."

"You could tell them that I didn't feel well and had to go home."

"They saw you crying, Jet. I know there's more to this than you're letting on." Her face softens. "You can tell—"

"There are things in my past that you don't understand."

She caresses my hand. "I'm sure the holidays are difficult for you as a widower. Christmas is hard for us, too, with my dad gone... He was the big patriarch of the family and now there's an empty seat every Christmas."

"There's more to it than that."

Her head tilts. "You can trust me with this," she says. "I won't judge you."

I pull Jay's picture from my wallet and push it across the table.

"Who's this?" she asks as she lifts the photo.

"His name is Jay."

Her eyes lock on the image like magnets. "Your nephew?"

"My son."

She struggles to respond.

"I thought you said you wouldn't judge," I say.

"I'm just surprised." She flips the photo around and reads the back. "I had no idea." She places it back into my open hand.

I return it to my wallet. I can tell that she doesn't know what to say now. She stares at me vacantly.

I break the silence. "He was a good kid. I was a terrible father," I say matter-of-factly. "I was the empty seat at almost every Christmas."

Tears unexpectedly shimmer in Linda's eyes. Her bottom lip quivers. "When did he pass? What happened?"

I shake my head. "Oh... no... he didn't pass..."

She wipes her eyes with a sleeve. "When was the last time you saw him, then?" she asks.

I think hard, my mind sifting through the memories. "It's been years... He's all grown up now..."

"What happened between you two?"

"He blames me." A searing knife digs into my chest. "He blames me for everything. He blames me for her death."

Horror develops in Linda's eyes. "But you didn't kill her."

I shake my head. "Not literally, no." I swallow hard. "I was the empty seat in more ways than one. I struck out looking with them every day that I wasn't there."

A long hush overcomes us once more. She drinks from her cup slowly and I continue picking at my scone.

It's Linda's turn to speak. "I think you need to go see him," she finally says.

"The last time we saw each other he said he didn't want to see me again," I reveal.

"He was probably just angry, Jet."

"I'm sure he was, but his words seemed final. I reached out once or twice after that, left some messages, but he never got back to me. I think he meant he didn't want to see me again... ever."

Linda reaches for my hand. "Things change. Time can change everything."

"So they say..." I want to believe her.

She can obviously tell I'm reluctant, so she pushes the topic: "Isn't it time to give it another try with your son?"

"Time to give it another swing?"

Linda nods. She leans over the table and takes hold of my other hand. She squeezes both of my hands and her eyes pierce me as always. She gives me a slight Janny-like smile. "Maybe his father's seat doesn't *need* to be empty."

# CHAPTER EIGHT

TEN-YEAR-OLD JAY climbs onto the pitcher's mound. I stand beside the bleachers on the first base side, unseen as I watch my son take a deep breath in his baggy uniform. He rests his heels on the rubber, concentrating squarely on the plate. He stares in to the catcher, his glove covering all but his eyes, and he shakes off a sign. I can tell he's fiddling with the ball in his glove, probably preparing to throw a curve. Little leaguers won't notice this. They're not looking for a pitcher tipping his pitches. I hope it goes unnoticed. I take a mental note: *Need to talk to him about tipping pitches...*

I study his mechanics as he takes a step back with his left foot, pivots his other foot flawlessly and kicks his left leg up high as practiced. He drives forward and lands hard on his left foot. He delivers the pitch with a grunt. His right leg swings around to join his left; his feet land parallel in the dirt at the front edge of the mound. He's in perfect fielding position as the ump raises a right hand to signal strike one. He winds up for his second pitch and his solid mechanics remain intact.

Strike two.

He delivers the third pitch, a fastball. The batter swings through the pitch, missing badly. I hear the coach yell from the dugout, "Good job, Jay!" I want to repeat that statement but don't want to draw any attention.

My cell vibrates in my pocket. I try to ignore it but it continues to buzz. I grab for it in my pocket, look at the screen. It's a reminder notification: **PRACTICE AT 12:45.** I misjudged the time. I need to leave in five minutes to beat the traffic to the stadium.

Jay steps back onto the rubber as the next batter approaches the batter's box. I can't concentrate; I can only think of tonight's game. Valentine throws a mean 12-6 curve and a splitter that drops by about a foot. His four-seamer clocks in at around 95-98 mph. And *he* doesn't telegraph his pitches.

I hear "strike!" in the background, but my focus remains on the game tonight. I need a three-hit game tonight to reach a .300 batting average. I'm not supposed to think about nor discuss my own stats but all players do. Some are just better actors or liars than others.

"Strike!"

I've lost track of the count, but I know I need to head to the car. I told Jay I'd take him out for ice cream after the game. I thought there would be time, I really did... I'll have to call Janice to ask her to pick him up.

I move away from the bleachers. I lumber over the uneven ground to the backstop behind home plate. I wave to Jay through the fence in between batters. He doesn't see me; his gaze stops at the catcher. Then his attention jumps to the next batter as he leaves the on-deck cir-cle and walks toward the plate. I wave again and this time Jay's eyes lock on me. I mouth, "I have to go. I'm sorry." I'm not sure that he can read my lips from here, so I point to my watch. Jay shakes his head and huffs.

I want to jump onto the field and explain that I miscalculated the time, that I'll take him out to ice cream next time, I promise, but he keeps shaking his head.

And now I'm late. I grudgingly turn my back to him and take the path to the parking lot. *He'll understand. Someday he'll understand.*

I reach the edge of the parking lot and hear a loud ping sound generated from an aluminum bat. I turn to the field as I backpedal toward my car. Jay drops his shoulders and his gaze follows the batter as he starts his trot around the bases. My heart sinks as I step into my car.

---

"Now boarding Flight 182... Yuma, Arizona..."

I stand from my chair and get into line on this long weekend. A couple people in line recognize me and nod. I release a half-hearted smile to each of them.

Linda's voice echoes in my mind, reassuring me: *"Maybe his father's seat doesn't need to be empty..."*

I've been following Jay's career from afar for years—his rise as an all-star high school pitcher, his development in college, his brush with single-A ball before his career-altering injury. I can see the video clip in my mind's eye of a grimacing Jay clutching at his elbow. I've probably watched that video from my apartment at least a dozen times. And now I picture him alone in Arizona mounting his baseball comeback in the Winter League, but this time I'm going to be there for him in person.

I board the plane and find an empty seat near the back. The seat I paid for with one of my nearly maxed out credit cards. The plane slowly fills. A father and young son sit in my row. His son sits in the window seat, grinning.

"Daddy, when will we get there?" the boy asks.

My heart grows heavy at the utterance of the word *Daddy.*

"We'll be there before you know it," the daddy responds with a smile.

The son peeks out the window as the plane takes off. The boy oohs and aahs as it reaches to the clouds and beyond, whirring through the air. All the while his daddy grins and eagerly points out landmarks from overhead.

After a few minutes, the boy rests his head on his daddy's shoulder, his eyes heavy. His eyes slowly shut. His daddy follows suit, a hand placed on his son's leg. I glance down at the bag by the daddy's feet and spot a blue **#1 DAD** hat poking out of the bag.

I sigh and then close my eyes, thinking of an adult Jay standing on the mound. He asks, "When will you be here?"

I respond, "I'll be there before you know it..."

———

I exit the hotel at nine o'clock in the morning. The warm air brushes over me. I look beyond the parking lot at the freshly trimmed palms bathing in the sun. The desert sand in the distance glows beneath the cloudless sky.

The shuttle pulls up in front of me, catching my attention. I ride the shuttle bus to the baseball field. We arrive at the fields. I leave the bus and walk to the entrance. RAY KROC BASEBALL COMPLEX in red stretches across a white sign over the front gates. I head to the will-call building, a light brown shoebox-like building with Plexiglas windows bordered by red molding.

I buy a ticket for Desert Sun Stadium where Jay will showcase his pitching talents to what will likely be a small crowd, in my experience. Mostly scouts looking for a diamond in the rough.

I sit at the top of the warm metal bleachers behind home plate. My large, thick sunglasses and trucker's hat conceal my identity as planned. I don't want to cause a distraction for Jay. The hat doesn't contain **#1 DAD** text, but I'm hopeful that one day it could... I gaze at the dark green and russet field as an anonymous onlooker, filling the once-empty seat that a son deserves to have filled.

About a dozen people occupy the seats down below. Netting encloses the section. Those closest to the field, in orange seats, hold radar guns and clipboards as they chat with one another.

The team takes the field. The umpires trail them. Jay strides to the mound and picks up the rosin bag. He tosses it up a couple times. His uniform is no longer baggy as in his younger years, and his hair reaches his neck beneath a green cap. He browses the infield as his teammates throw the ball back and forth, readying themselves for the game.

The center fielder, meanwhile, tosses the ball from one outfielder to the other, the fence behind them decorated with advertisements— a sign for a cable company, Mexican restaurant, beer, and bunch of local companies.

Jay drops the rosin bag. **BRINE** on the back of his Long Beach gray and green jersey causes me to smile beneath my getup. He steps onto the rubber as he has thousands of times before.

The PA announcer's voice floods the field with "Play ball!" Then he announces the first batter as "Larry Demetrius." He enters the batter's box and glares at Jay. Jay returns the look.

The first pitch sizzles through the air and pops the glove on the outside corner for a strike. I look down at the orange seat area, to the men with raised radar guns. I can't see the guns' readings from up here, but that looked and sounded at least 90 mph. The scouts whisper among themselves and scribble notes on their clipboards.

The second pitch arrives, a second strike, this time swinging. Less of a *pop* this time and much more movement. Definitely a breaking ball, and Jay didn't telegraph it. The dozens of fans throughout the ball field start to clap. The claps echo in the empty stands.

Jay hurls the third pitch of the at bat—a called strike three, that old backwards K. I hear a couple cheers and some jeers. My hand begins to shake. My heart races. I quietly remind myself that I'm a bystander. Just a bystander. I breathe in and out. In and out...

Jay pitches six shutout innings. In the seventh, a second baseman takes Jay deep, a solo shot. Jay's shoulders don't sag. He doesn't appear discouraged. He simply motions for the catcher to throw him the ball. My boy is a man now.

My back isn't turned, and I'm not walking to my car this time. I don't have any other game to attend. I'm present. I'm a dad now.

He strikes out the remaining batters in the inning, totaling eight strikeouts through seven. The scouts continue to chatter and write their notes.

He gives up a hit in the eighth and another hit in the ninth but strikes out three more. 2-1 flashes on the scoreboard in centerfield as the final score. A light clap reverberates in the stands.

I keep my eyes locked on Jay as he walks to the dugout. I make my way through the aisles, down to the dugout. I hang out behind the dugout awaiting my chance. I wait for what seems like an eternity. Then it happens—he steps out of the dugout and turns slowly in my direction. His eyes meet mine. I remove my sunglasses and hat. His eyes bulge, then he swings around. He stands still with his back turned to me, literally turning his back on me. He exhales loudly.

I consider giving up, but then I blurt out his name. I hope for a miracle. I hope for *something.*

He faces me again, walks toward the fence in between us. He wears a deadpan expression. "Hi, Jet," he says unemotionally.

His words stab at me. I struggle to respond to his coldness.

"Can I help you?" he asks sharply, leaning in.

"I just wanted to see you play, son." My voice shakes. "Just wanted to talk with you. No strings attached."

"So... what did the great Jet Brine think of my performance?" His voice tinged with sarcasm.

Without hesitation, "You were amazing."

I don't know if he expected criticism or what, but Jay's face instantly flushes scarlet. "Let's hope the scouts thought so, too." He motions to the orange seats.

"I'm sure they did," I say promptly.

"This isn't exactly my dream, you know, to be playing out here."

"I wouldn't think so."

A teammate calls his name. Jay raises a pointer finger to him. "I'll be right there," he says.

I lean in closer to the fence. "I'm sorry to show up unannounced," I say. "I'm not here to cause you strife. I just didn't know how else to reach you. I want to spend time with you. It's been too long."

Jay crosses his arms, says nothing.

"I flew all this way. . ." My voice breaks. "At least have lunch with me. Hear me out."

He raises his eyebrows, surveying my face. Opens his mouth to speak, then closes it. Finally, he says, "Tomorrow. For lunch." He describes a nearby restaurant and says he'll meet me there at noon. He steps away from the fence. He shouts out his cell phone number to use in case anything changes, and I memorize it. It's a new number. He gives me one final parting glance and then joins his teammate.

I leave the field with cautious optimism.

# CHAPTER NINE

"YOU AND I WERE SUPPOSED to have a nice dinner together." Janice slams her hand on the granite counter of our kitchen island. The freshly cut vegetables fly off the cutting board and scatter over the counter next to the knife. "You're like a ghost to me!"

"I'm here now," I say, my voice defensive. The grip on my cell phone strengthens as the cell continues to vibrate.

She tears the polka dot apron off her body and throws it on the tile floor. "Here I am trying to make a home-cooked meal for the two of us and it's 1-800-Jet. Can't you just shut that thing off for a moment?"

She hastily removes the boiling pot from the stove and dumps the water down the sink.

My phone pulsates again. I look at the screen, at the numerous text messages.

"The skipper needs me to come in to watch some video on last night's game," I try to explain calmly. I look up at her. "Apparently, he found a hitch in my swing. That would explain my recent slump. It's correctable, but he wants to show me the details in a short meeting. A meeting now."

Her nostrils flare.

"I told you I'll be back tonight," I say. "It's not a big deal." I lean over the counter.

She turns and stares vacantly at the window over the sink.

"Jay's curfew is at 10." She points at the ornate wall clock that reads 7:39. "There goes our romantic evening together..." Her tone strained. She glares at me, her eyes bloodshot.

"We can do this another time, then," I say casually.

She bangs her fist on the counter. "It's always next time with you. We'll have dinner *next time*," she says, her voice laced with fury. "We'll go out *next time*. Spend time with friends *next time*."

My fingers tap the granite. "Overreacting again," I say. "Can't you dial it down a notch for once?" *She must be off her meds today... Here we go again...*

She wags her head, issues a snort of disgust. "I don't know what to say to you right now."

"For once!" I can't stand to be in the room with her for another moment.

"You know what, on second thought... why don't you just stay where you're *really* going this evening." Her speech wavers. "Stay there and don't come back tonight."

I grab my Benz keys from a pocket. "I don't know why you're being so accusatory. I'm meeting with the skipper. End of story." I leave the house with a slam of the door for emphasis. My jet-black Benz roars down our street bordered by gated properties. The ten-minute drive feels long. I arrive at the clubhouse and enter the skipper's office.

Sitting in his high-backed chair, he peers over a sheet of paper. "Ah, Jet! Join me." He places the paper onto a large stack of papers to his left, then faces a nearby computer screen on his mahogany desk. He waves me over to the screen. We watch the film repeatedly. He wants me to start off in my batting stance with the bat resting on my shoulder. "Swing from the shoulder straight through," he says. "Don't drop those hands, not even an inch."

Then he shows me a clip from Cal Ripken Jr.'s career, how his batting stance evolved over time. Ripken's black bat rests directly on his shoulder. He slides the bat back and forth over his shoulder to remind himself to keep the bat there prior to the swing. This results in a completely level swing with no hitch.

"I don't want you to be married to a particular stance, Jet," the skipper says. "If Ripken can change his stance, so you can you." He clicks off the videos. "Give it a try for a week and let's reconnect at that point to compare the results."

The meeting lasts for about an hour. I don't want to go back home right away. I consider booking a hotel suite for the night, away from the delusional Janice. The Marriot always treats me well on these occasions. Michael the manager is endlessly accommodating. He always ensures I receive the VIP treatment whenever I need a place to stay to escape the wrath of Janice.

After some thought, I instead drop by the casino for a quick fix. *What will it hurt?* I spend a grand on the slots, chump change. Casino workers and customers recognize me, eyes rounded with excitement, and they clap as my slot machine flashes. Within an hour, I triple my money. *Money making money.* My worries melt away for a moment. I'd love to continue playing through the night, but then, as the erratic Janice enters my thoughts, I'm reminded of the doc's stern warning from months ago. "Janice is not to stop her meds cold turkey again. It could be dangerous."

I grudgingly leave the casino. *I could've won so much more but I need to talk with Janice about her medication.* I take my time driving home, below the posted speed limit. I listen to jazz and drum my fingers on the steering wheel.

I pull up to the house. Light shines through nearly every window. *She's still up. What's going on with her?* I don't know how I'll segue into a conversation about her meds, and I fear that the talk could lead to another fight, but I know it needs to be discussed for her sake... and mine.

I unlock the front door, and push it open. I hear faint music playing overhead, upstairs. I cross through the living room, to the kitchen. She hasn't cleaned up from earlier. The apron remains on the floor, the veggies strewn over the counter.

I walk back through the living room. I call her name up the stairs. She doesn't answer. The light music continues playing. I figure she's probably taking one of her long baths in the jacuzzi tub. *If it helps her mood, then fine by me.* I shrug, then plop onto our couch in front of the expansive TV. It flickers on with a touch of the remote. *SportsCenter* plays. The talking heads discuss the latest player acquisitions from several baseball teams.

I zone out and tire of the show. I flip through the channels. *Jay should be home soon... Maybe I'll watch a sitcom to kill some time. I could use a laugh for a few minutes.* I can't find anything to my liking, so I power off the TV. I decide that I should finally confront Janice about her erratic behavior before Jay returns.

I climb the hardwood stairs. The volume of the music rises with each step. I scan our master bedroom, and see her clothing scattered over the carpeted floor, leading to the bathroom. I follow the trail of clothes toward the bathroom. I hear running water. Trickling water. I step into the room with socked feet. My feet land in a pool of red water; my socks quickly absorb the liquid. My eyes follow the puddle up to the overflowing tub. I wobble toward the tub. I step over a bloody kitchen knife, giving it a double-take as I pass it. I notice Janice's gashed arm draped over the side of the tub, blood spilling down the outside of the porcelain, her head bobbing face-up in the red water.

I rip a towel off a nearby rack, and wrap the white towel around her forearm. I press on the towel. I turn off the faucet with the other hand. I hover over my sweet Janny's limp body. I grab her shoulder and shake, water splashing up at me. Her eyes open a crack. She moans but can't seem to speak. I wince, wet hand reaching into my pocket for my phone.

"Oh, my God, Janny!"

I call 9-1-1, describe the emergency, my voice wavering. Her eyes close again. I quickly reach into the tub and pull the drain plug. I return my hand to her towel briefly, and press on it, applying pressure to her wound. The red-tinged water swirls down the drain.

I prop her naked body up with one hand and hold onto the phone with the other. I kneel to the tub, put my head on her forehead. Tears roll off my face and onto hers. "Janny, stay with me... Promise me you'll stay right here with me."

She mumbles something indiscernible, her bare chest rising and falling, rising and falling...

The doorbell rings minutes later. I take long strides through the receding water, out of the bathroom. I careen down the stairs to the front door, leaving a painted trail of fluid in my wake.

"Direct me to her, please," one of the paramedics says calmly. I point toward the stairs. I follow him and another paramedic up the stairs. I guide them to the bathroom, shrinking at the thought of them seeing her bloodied nude body.

I stand in the hallway, waiting. Sounds of footsteps come from the stairs. I look over at the staircase, see a couple police officers stepping onto the top steps in the hallway. They glance at me. I point to the bathroom without uttering a word. They enter the bathroom and speak in muffled voices. I hear splashing and I hear her groan once more. The paramedics carry her blanketed body out of the bathroom on a stretcher, the police trailing behind. With little effort, the paramedics lift her down the stairs.

The police wave me down outside as the paramedics lift Janice into the ambulance. An officer asks for my statement. "We had a fight,"

I say, trembling. "I came home and found her like that—all cut up with the kitchen knife." He wants to know her date of birth, my whereabouts before the incident. I give the date and give a detailed time line of my evening. He asks if she left a note. I shake my head. Then he asks if she has a history of mental illness. I nod, fearful of mentioning it. Guilt floods me. *If I would've just come home sooner.*

"Do you know the name of her doctor?" asks the other officer. "We'll need to touch base with her doctor to confirm your statement." I give the name, the office address and the meds Janice just quit taking. That satisfies them finally.

I ride in the ambulance with Janice. I sit behind her stretcher. Her chest moves up and down beneath the blanket. I call Jay, explain the situation. He cries and yells into the phone, says he can be at the hospital in an hour, that he's a couple towns over with his friends.

"The one night you're late for curfew and you chose *this* night?" I say firmly, restraining myself.

"I'll... I'll be there." He hangs up.

Men and women in white coats and scrubs meet us at the emergency room door and wheel Janice away. A nurse hangs around briefly and addresses me, with words like "critical condition" and "emergency surgery." She asks me to sign some paperwork, handing me a pen and a clipboard.

I sit in the waiting area with elbows on my knees. Jazz music plays over the speakers. The music doesn't create its intended calming feeling; it sparks rage inside of me. *The warnings were there. I should have been there. Maybe I could have stopped her if I didn't decide to play the slots!* I feel sick to my stomach at the thought.

Jay bursts through the entryway and runs to me. I stand, try to hug him. He pulls away, face red and furious.

"Where is she?" He glowers at me.

"She's in surgery."

He drops into a seat, looks down at the floor. He doesn't say another word, averting his eyes from me. Light jazz continues, boiling my blood.

The automatic entry doors open and close as time whirls by. People cross the waiting room as streaks of color. I hear muffled voices, faint cries from a child, and continuous beeping from somewhere. I nearly black out, thinking of Janny in the tub, her flaccid body. *She just wanted me around...*

Doctor Anchele stops in front of me. "She's stable," he reveals. "You and your son can visit her momentarily." Jay overhears the doctor. Silently, he stands and starts pacing around the room, avoiding me.

I walk the long corridor minutes later, Jay trailing me. I fill the seat next to her bed. Jay sits near her feet. I inspect her forearm covered in gauze, nose tubes resting against her ashen skin. My sweet Janny gasps for air as her eyes open. She slowly blinks at me, opens her mouth to speak. She releases a breath instead. Her machines blink and beep steadily by her bed. She turns her head, looks me over, her once vibrant eyes now tired and swollen.

"I'm sorry..." she breathes.

I hold her hand lightly. Jay sobs at her feet, face in his hands.

"I didn't... mean any of it," Janice continues. Her eyes go blank, life ebbing from them. Her eyelids shut and her hand goes limp.

I squeeze her hand. No response. The beeping of the machines suddenly shifts into a loud alarm-like tone. I jump out of my seat. A nurse runs into the room, followed by a doctor. Jay wails like a wounded animal as they place the pads on her chest, attempting to restart her heart.

It's too late.

———

I settle into the red-cushioned booth at noon sharp. The waitress comes over to the table. "Would you like to start with a drink?" she asks.

I order a Pepsi. "My son should be here any minute, too," I add. She gives a lopsided grin and walks off.

I rest my elbows on the checkered table. I start to wonder if he'll show up. I realize I don't deserve anything from grown-up Jay, but a no-show from him would devastate me.

The waitress drops off the bubbling glass, and shoots a pity smile my way. *I look like an idiot...* I take some sips, nibble at the straw. I gander at my watch every couple of minutes, tapping a toe on the floor. The door groans open. I look up. It isn't him. A bald, middle-aged mustached man walks in and seats himself in the corner of the restaurant.

The door swings open once again. Jay appears in the doorway wearing a blue polo shirt, his biceps bulging. He looks at me, his eyes showing some level of surprise. His eyebrows waggle. He adjusts his cap. I fear that he'll turn around and walk away, repaying me for the times I seemingly abandoned him. His eyes narrow as he walks with a swagger to my table. I wonder if he's trying to put on a show for me, overcompensating for his sadness or anger.

He fills the seat across from me. He puts his elbows on the table. Mimicking me? Mocking me?

"I honestly don't know what we have to discuss." He doesn't waste any time. "Why are you *really* in Arizona? Here on business or something?" His words claw at my throat. He touches the brim of his baseball cap. I guess his response makes sense; he's accustomed to my treating him like an afterthought.

"I'm here for *you*." I place my hand on his. He pulls his hand away, removes his arms from the table.

"Well, that's something new," he scoffs. "I guess an old dog *can* learn new tricks, huh?"

"I see you've learned a few yourself... Baseball-wise, I mean... You've got one heck of a four-seamer, Jay."

The compliment rolls off him; he seems unwilling to accept praise from me today. "Now if only the right people would notice it," he says.

"I'm proud of you," I say earnestly. "Your mom would be proud of you, too."

"My mom?" His voice sharpens. "If you didn't treat her like an unwanted dog, maybe she'd still be here to see me play." I've heard different variations of this throughout the years. His face reddens. "Ever think of that?" he asks.

"I think about that every day." I look down at the table, unable to look him in the eyes. "Every hour of every day." Silence falls over the table.

The waitress joins us at the table. She takes our order and flits away.

"I remember the first time I played catch with you," I say fondly, my eyes meeting his. "You had this little plastic glove. Do you remember?" He nods reluctantly. "You were four or five, somewhere around that age, and your mom watched from the garden. She had this big smile. You know the one..." I hear Jay sigh. I continue, "And I could feel her eyes on you as I showed you how to hold the glove just right... I lobbed the ball to you and you caught nearly every throw."

The red on his face dissipates. "And she gave me this big round of applause from the garden, like I had won the championship," Jay recalls.

"She loved seeing us play ball. Do you remember what she called me?"

"Coach Papa..." He says in a soft tone.

I smile. "Coach Papa."

The waitress places our plates on the table. Jay digs into his sandwich. I take a couple bites of mine.

I can't hold back, so I say, "I'm sorry, son." I stare into his shocked eyes. His forehead puckers. "I'm so sorry. You're right. I should have been more attentive. I should have been a better husband, a better father. A dad." I gasp for air. "I wasn't there for either of you often enough..."

Jay just looks at me blankly.

"I'm sorry every day. Every hour of every day."

Jay's eyes widen and begin to glisten. Silence surrounds us for a moment. He sniffs. "I have an idea," he says faintly.

I incline my head. "What is it?"

"Meet me outside at my car." He stands and walks outside.

I wave the waitress down and pay the bill. I dart to the door and step outside. I see Jay standing at his open trunk holding two baseball gloves. He tosses one to me under the noonday sun. He steps to the desert dirt behind the paved parking lot. I do the same.

"Here you go, Coach Papa," he says as he throws me the new baseball. It pops into my glove.

He shows me his two-seamer. It nearly knocks the glove off my hand. We laugh together.

"Do you mind if I come to your game again tomorrow?" I ask amid throws.

He pauses with the ball in hand. "Yeah... I think I'd like that."

I can feel Janny's eyes on us, her warmth filling me up, as she smiles down on us from her garden somewhere above.

# CHAPTER TEN

I CLIMB INTO MY HOTEL BED, and pull the sheets up to my chest. My heart starts racing. I notice a touch of nausea but figure it must be the fried food from dinner not settling well. *I don't do well with fried foods. I should have known better.*

The feeling will pass.

I think of playing catch with Jay earlier today in the bright desert sun. Joy bubbles up inside of me, but the nausea increases and displaces the happiness.

The feeling doesn't pass.

I stagger to the bathroom as if drunk. Another wave of nausea overtakes me. I try to force down the sick feeling. I gag. I retch, bitterness filling my mouth. My skin crawls and I grow cold. The sickness keeps me awake all night.

Sunlight stretches its shining fingers through the hotel room window. Guilt torments me as I lie at the base of the toilet, realizing that there's no way I'll be able to attend Jay's game today as promised. I lift my weak body off the floor, shivering, and I grab my cell in the other room.

I call the number Jay gave me. It rings three times and he answers in a groggy voice. "What's up?"

I lift myself onto the bed. "I'm sick." Embarrassment and shame wash over me. "I'd love to see you today but I must have eaten something bad last night. I was up all night."

"Okay..." Jay says in a skeptical tone.

Inwardly, I wince. "Really, it's terrible. I wanted to see you today, but—"

"I guess it doesn't surprise me," he says. Jay's disappointed voice shreds my insides. Then his voice turns hostile, "Of course you haven't changed..." He pauses. "I don't know what I was thinking."

"I swear to you, I wanted to be there this time." I interject.

He hangs up on me. I ball up into the fetal position on the bed, face contorting and eyes swimming with tears. My stomach continues to roil. I think about giving up, but overwhelming guilt forces me to call him again.

It rings once, twice, three times. Goes to voice mail.

Determined not to go down without swinging, I call once more. I land in his voicemail straightaway. I leave a long-winded message apologizing profusely, explaining that the sickness is for real, that it's probably the worst food poisoning or stomach bug I've ever had and it came at the worst possible time.

I eventually pass out on the bed.

I awake to a text from him. It reads:

I'm sure your "sickness" is complete BS and ur just exhausted from last night's gambling binge. I've seen this crap from you too many times to ignore it now. I'm done. Leave me alone.

Our fragile relationship shatters with that text. My stomach churns some more. I don't know what I could have done differently this time. I can't get out of bed. A mix of anger and sadness thunders through me. I'm barely able to breathe, the fear of never seeing him again tightening my chest.

I whimper and cry myself back to sleep. I have a short dream that consists of Jay standing over my bed. He sees me balled up and he notices the wet sheets from all my tears and he realizes that I'm for real this time. I didn't come up with some lame excuse to avoid spending time with him.

I awake again to the nightmare that is my life. I frantically call him and I land in his voice mail once more. I leave a quick message of desperation, this time explaining that my flight leaves tomorrow, that I don't know how I'll get on that plane unless I'm feeling much better. I tell him that I'd love to see him before I leave Arizona, body willing.

I lie in bed all day. I drink numerous bottles of water from the minibar. I eat some crackers, too. I flip through the channels on the small flat-screen TV mounted on the wall. I stop on a Lifetime movie. Some sappy flick about a guy trying to win back his girlfriend. In a brief montage, he plays his guitar outside her window. He sends her roses and chocolates. He sends her love notes. He calls her and leaves adoring messages. Nothing works.

My scalp prickles with shame as I think of Jay at his game without me. There's no cute montage playing for us. He's there alone. Coach Papa is nowhere to be seen, as usual. I attempt to get out of bed and I nearly fall over due to the dizziness. I want to go see him, to make an appearance somehow, but my body doesn't allow me.

The next morning, I wake up at six o'clock, my stomach calm. I check my phone. No messages, no texts from Jay. I hope that he'll get in touch before my flight at noon. False hope, I'm sure. I don't know where he is at this hour. If I knew, I'd go there now. I send him a text. It bounces back as "message cannot be delivered." My stomach drops down to my feet.

I wobble downstairs and gather myself a small continental breakfast. I force myself to eat a quarter of a plain bagel. It's dry and taste-less, but I need to eat something before my flight. I check my cell repeatedly as I sit on one of the plastic chairs in the breakfast room. No messages.

I walk slowly back up to my room, slightly hunched over. I call him for what seems like the hundredth time and I hear an out of ser-vice recording. I call again and encounter the same recording. He's either disconnected his phone or blocked me. The latter is more likely.

A weight settles on my heart as I start to pack my belongings.

———————

I arrive back east in the evening. I throw my bags on the floor near the door and plop onto my small bed. I look to my cell, wanting to delete Jay's awful text message. I can't will myself to delete it. I cringe at the thought that this could be the last time I hear from him. The words "gambling binge" cause my skin to tingle with excitement or maybe anger, I'm not sure. *If that's what he thinks of me, I might as well play the part.*

As one of the walking dead, I leave my apartment and get into my car. I drive through the packed-down snow and ice. I drive fast. I don't mind death. I'd greet it now as I would an old friend. Maybe I should just turn the wheel and drive myself straight into the trees. *Who would miss old washed-up Jet Brine, anyway?*

Linda's face smiles in my mind. I shake off the image, resentment building in my heart. *It was her idea. She pushed me to reach out to Jay.* My hands tighten around the steering wheel as I continue to accelerate.

I arrive at the casino unharmed. As I get out of the car, I grab at my stomach. It's still sore. Warmth spreads through my body as I reach the casino entrance, my temple. I go to the on-site ATM and withdraw several hundred dollars, nearly emptying my account.

I spot the slot machines. Longing whispers through me. I'm like that creature from *Lord of the Rings*, the one whose eyes sparkle whenever he sees or hears of the ring. I sit on a red bench before one of the slots.

I feed the machine for hours, repeatedly pulling down on the silver handle, watching the icons spin.

Bells and whistles sound somewhere behind me, somewhere out of sight. "Yes!" a woman shouts.

And then, hours later, the bells and whistles finally sound directly overhead. I pump a fist in the air. *Jackpot!*

I feel breathless. I flicker to life, resurrected. I stand, my knees weakened. Outwardly, I play it cool, but internally, I'm electrified by the win. It's like the feeling of hitting a home run.

---

I scoot through the entrance at work. I sneak to my desk a half-hour late. Egg-loving Fred takes notice as he leans back in his chair from his cubicle next door. He looks at me, pointing to his Mickey Mouse watch.

*Who does this guy think he is?* I think to myself.

Fred slinks to the manager's office a few minutes later when he thinks I'm not watching. He's like a child about to tattle in the schoolyard. I realize that I need to look busy, so I lean forward and take an order from one of my bins. I start entering the order mindlessly. I stop, rest a hand on my front pants pocket, over the thick wallet, to remind myself of last night's winnings. To remind myself that it wasn't a dream.

Then I hear breathing behind my back. I turn and Holly's eyes burn into me. She crosses her arms. "We need to have another talk," she says.

---

Linda asks me out to a movie. I commit to it and then cancel last minute, passive-aggressive. She sighs over the phone after I tell her that I forgot about some prior commitments. I'm sure my vagueness raises suspicion.

I return to the casino instead. I visit the same slot machine as before. A couple of the casino workers recognize me; their faces twist into smiles at the sight of me.

I feed the ravenous machine. To my right sits an old, hunched woman with a cane by her side. She reminds me of a chewed-up version of Linda's mother.

She gazes at me. "You're the guy who hit the jackpot, huh?" she asks in a raspy voice.

I don't recognize her from that night, but I guess she remembers me. It's nice to be recognized as a winner for once. "Yeah, that's me," I say.

She runs a hand through her long gray hair. "So, what's a handsome guy like you doing here alone?"

I cringe, thinking of Linda. I shrug my shoulders.

She continues toying at a lock of her hair. "Well, do you have a girl?" Her eyelashes flutter.

I want to puke. "Yeah."

She turns away, annoyed. "The cute ones are always taken," she says beneath her breath.

I lose four hundred fifty-eight dollars after five hours. I'm tempted to keep going but I'm hungry. The starving machine will have to wait until my return.

———

Linda invites me to a fancy dinner with her friends. I show up at the restaurant about twenty minutes late, having gambled through the night. Embarrassment coils around me.

"Good of you to join us." Tammy, one of her friends, jokes. She stares at me beneath long, fringed lashes.

I slouch in my seat, shoulders slumped.

Linda's cheeks turn pink. "Now, now... I'm sure he has a reasonable explanation. Right, Jet? Traffic?"

I blot my forehead with a handkerchief. "Right," I say.

Her other friend, Cassandra, speaks from across the table. "A man of many words..." She chortles. Then she fiddles with one of her gold earrings.

Her friends chuckle as I try to order my dinner. I can't pronounce all the items on the elaborate menu, so I stumble over a few of the words as I attempt to relay the information to the steely-eyed waitress.

I want to disappear from this place. I'd rather be at the slots, even if that means sitting next to the old, flirtatious cane-bearer from last night.

---

Valentine's Day appears from out of nowhere, amid all the gambling and late nights. I stop at a CVS on my way to Linda's. I enter the candy aisle. Two other men roam the aisle, their eyes listless. One of the men, a portly fellow, yanks a box of candies from the nearly empty shelf. It's the last box of high-end candies, and he holds it close to his chest, as if I'm going to try to rip it away from him.

The other man lifts a white teddy bear from the shelf. He gives me a frosty look. Stone-cold.

I examine the understocked shelves. I don't know what to get Linda, the woman with everything. I guess this is what I deserve for waiting until last minute. The barren shelves stare back at me. I grab a small box of candies.

Linda inspects the small box with glossy eyes after I present them to her at her front door. She frowns as she discovers this is her one and only gift. I want to curl up in shame.

# CHAPTER ELEVEN

**I'VE BEEN SITTING IN THE ROOM** with the glass-covered walls for the past five minutes, Maggy of HR and my boss, Holly, interrogating me. Maggy, untidy as ever, wears a mustard stain on her blouse today. Poor Maggy needs to start bringing a change of clothes to work. Holly sits to her right, arms folded over the table.

"Mr. Brine," Maggy says, all cop-like, "as I said, I took a risk on you. You struck me as a man of integrity and values. But over the course of the last week—*and don't deny it*—you've been late to work nearly each and every day." She passes a time card across the table. "As you can see there, we have definitive proof of your continuous tardiness."

"And this is a fireable offense, as far as I'm concerned," Holly chimes in.

"Yes," Maggy continues, "and, in most cases, you'd be terminated at this point in time. However, a certain higher-up individual has vouched for you and has implored us to give you another chance. We've decided to defer to her judgment as of now." Her glasses slip down her nose.

Holly weighs in again as the cop routine continues: "But that's not to say that you're totally off the hook, Jet. This is as official as official gets." She wags her pointer finger at me. "One more time and your employment will be terminated."

*Terminated.* I wince. *They make it sound so serious, like a death sentence, a ride in the electric chair.*

"Do you have anything to say?" Holly inquires sternly.

"I'm really very sorry. I've had some late nights dealing with a personal matter." I decide to omit the part about the slots. "It won't happen again."

I bang on Linda's front door in the cold darkness of night. She opens the door a crack, peeks through, guarded. She recognizes me and swings the door open. She smiles, says, "Oh, I'm glad you're here. I was just preparing dinner," but I move past her, into the kitchen.

I plant myself in front of her stove, an immovable force. "I can't believe you did that!"

She squints at me from the kitchen doorway. "Why are you shouting?"

"I know it was you. I don't need you to intercede on my behalf. I'm a big boy."

"Listen, you'd be unemployed right now if I hadn't intervened," she says, her voice booming. She softens a bit. "If anything, you should be thanking me."

"Well, if you had actually approached me about any of this, you would have discovered that I don't really need this job or the money."

"So, you're self-sabotaging, then?" She wags her head. "And what do you mean by *you don't need the money?*" She grinds her jaw.

I remove my thick wallet and toss it onto the counter. "Take a look for yourself." I point to the wallet. "And there's more where that came from, too."

She moves away from the doorway, the clicks of her heels echoing off the marble floor. She opens the wallet. To her surprise she finds a fat stack of hundred-dollar bills. She pulls the stack from the wallet, fanning it out. "What's this all about?" she asks. "I had a feeling you had gotten yourself into something. You haven't been acting like yourself lately. You've been so unreliable."

"Geez, thanks for the compliment."

"Please tell me it isn't drugs."

I let out a quick chuckle. "I won it, actually."

She returns the money to the wallet. "Gambling? Is this gambling money?"

"Yeah. I finally won big."

"I thought you were done with gambling. Is this why you've been out late night after night?"

"Aren't you happy for me?"

"Happy that you won some money, but nearly lost your steady job?" She puffs out her breath.

"And you've basically neglected your girlfriend, you know," she adds. "No, not happy at all."

I'm about to roar at her, but then I spot the items on another counter: the diced veggies strewn on the cutting board and the knife responsible. I start to quake, remembering the horrifying scene from years ago—Janice's kitchen knife on the bathroom floor and her blood-spattered body in the tub. *If only I had gone straight home instead of playing the slots...*

"Are you okay?" Linda wraps an arm around me. She leans in. "Jet, are you all right?" she asks worriedly.

The thought of Janice in the hospital bed blazes into my mind like a fastball. I see and hear young Jay crying out after she flatlines. I think of all that was holy to me up to that point: the money and the gambling and the baseball. I recall adult Jay voicing his displeasure by way of his recent statement, "Of course you haven't changed... What was I thinking?"

I crumble to my knees on the cold kitchen floor and start bawling. Linda joins me on her knees. She shakes my shoulders. "Jet, what's wrong? Tell me what's wrong," she says, frantic.

"I failed her." My vision blurs. "I failed him. I failed them both."

"I don't understand..."

I finally tell her about my trip to Arizona to see Jay, and then: "It was a total disaster." My heart wrenches. "He still thinks I'm a loser..." Something shatters inside of me, like glass against a hammer. "He still doesn't want anything to do with me."

"Take some deep breaths," she says. "In and out, in and out."

I follow her advice. Repeatedly, I draw in a long breath and then blow out my cheeks. After a minute, my breathing normalizes. We stand together.

"You need to take a swing at this one," she says. "You need some help."

I know she's right, but I hate that. The slot machines call for me from afar, but I try to block it out.

She takes in a sharp breath. "Gamblers Anonymous," she breathes out. "You have to get this under control. It's destroying you." She holds my hand, her eyes glowing with affection. "It's destroying *us*..."

# CHAPTER TWELVE

**WE SIT IN A CIRCLE** of metal folding chairs in the cool basement of the church. The smell of mold and mothballs and desperation overwhelm me. I want to get up and run away. I scan the group and the broad-shouldered group leader, Stan, gives me a reassuring smile. No doubt he can tell that I'm uncomfortable.

I fold my hands in my lap.

A young woman across the circle, wearing a long ponytail and eighties-style fluorescent clothing, nibbles on her fingernails.

A man to her right is slumped in his chair, looking at the stained carpet. His all-black baseball hat covers his eyes almost entirely. I guess he wants to remain truly anonymous.

Whenever I gave Gamblers Anonymous any thought in the past, I always supposed I'd appear in some disguise—like sunglasses and maybe a hat like the guy over there—as I sometimes do in public. But I figured this morning, in a moment of reflection, that we're all in the same boat in here, and it's supposed to be anonymous anyway, so there's no need to throw on a costume.

I continue scanning the circle. Everyone appears basically normal, if there is such a thing. I think of the most common names like John and Jane and Nancy and Bob and those could very well be the names of these people.

The woman with the ponytail, Natalie, is the first to share today. She admits, in a high-pitched voice, that she took out a loan recently to fund a night at the casino.

"I knew better but I couldn't control it," she adds as she slouches in her chair. "I've won big before, and that keeps me coming back." Her clothes nearly blind me as I look on.

She goes on to explain that she's racked up all sorts of debt due to her addiction, that she's maxed out almost every credit card, and some months—when she "loses big"—she doesn't have enough money for food and other essentials.

"I know gambling's a terrible habit and it does me no good," she says. "I've gone two weeks without gambling. I can't promise I won't go back but at least this is a start." She raises a triumphant arm. "Two weeks."

The group gives her a round of applause like she's won an award.

Stan addresses the group in a husky voice, "I'd like to use this moment to remind everyone here that regardless of the outcome, gambling is never the solution. As I've said many times before, gambling is mostly used as an escape, a way to cover up emotional distress, and many of us experience dire consequences from our gambling. It's a terrible condition and it's never worth it."

Stan points to a white-bearded man with a leathery face. "Would you like to share?" he asks.

The man speaks in a southern drawl, "I was fixin' to stay in the other night. I had the TV on watchin' some ladies dance around in their skivvies." He pauses. "I promise, I ain't no perv." He fidgets in his seat. "A no-good gambler, yes, but a perv, no. Y'all know."

A couple of the attendees chuckle and giggle.

"No judgment here," Stan interjects in monotone.

"Then a commercial popped on that darn idiot box," the southern man proceeds. "And wouldn't cha know it, some fast-talkin' slick-willy says, 'Come on down and get your game on,' and he was pointin' at the Black Jack table." He hooks his gleaming black shoes around the chair legs as he takes a breath. "But I'll tell y'all, I didn't get my 'game on' that night. Heck, I got up a few times to head to the door, I ain't gonna lie. But I didn't go. Two years free of gamblin' and I ain't goin' back now." He leans back in his chair. He lifts his chin. "Bless my heart." He puts his hands behind his head, obviously proud of himself.

A gentle titter rolls through the group.

Stan holds up a hand. The chuckling sub-sides. He nods at the man with the black hat. "Care to share?" he asks.

The man shrugs, seemingly indifferent about the idea. "I guess," he says as he sits up in the seat. "What am I supposed to say?"

"Whatever comes to mind," Stan says. "Anything relating to your condition."

He adjusts the brim of his hat. I can see his eyes poking through now. "I sold my Rolex last week," the man says. "Pawned it for half its value. And of course, I ended up at the track." I await some sort of gambling success story, but he says, "I lost all of it. Every last penny, gone..."

No one claps.

Then Stan's sausage finger points my way. "And you?"

I don't want to hold back. Something about the supposed anonymity of the group, and the fact that no one here seems to recognize me, causes me to take a leap: "Well, I've been gam-bling for years. Mostly slots. Won some, lost some. Won big recently—"

"Again, it's not about the outcome," Stan reminds us.

"Right…" I nod. "Gambling's caused all sorts of issues for me. It's hurt pretty much everyone in my life, at some point or another including me. I used to be a real high roller, which basically just meant that I had a greater fall."

I lock eyes with the southern man; he's stroking his beard, pondering. I explain my recent tardiness to work and the resulting official warning. I hear some sighs from the group.

"And my son," I say, and I can hardly believe I'm about to share this, "my son thinks I'm the same loser as before and wants nothing to do with me." I tell them about my trip to Arizona and how I couldn't make it to Jay's second game because I fell sick after eating some bad food the night before. "He thought I had been up all night gambling." I exhale loudly. "I hadn't been, but I guess I can't blame him for thinking it." Embarrassment stirs inside of me as the strangers in the circle eye me.

After the meeting, as I am about to exit the church, I hear the southern accent from behind, "Hey, you."

I turn around and face the smiling man. He comes closer; his breath smells of peppermint. "I reckon you'll need some one-on-one help," he says. He shakes my hand with a strong grip. "You can call me Boone. I ain't got no last name that you need to know." He winks. "Boone will do just fine."

"Name's Jet." I take a step back.

"All right, *Name's Jet*," he jokes, "here's my number." He hands me an index card from his breast pocket. I look down at the card.

"Call that number day or night," he says. "Anytime you're fixin' to hit the slots, you just ring that number and holler at me, ya hear?"

I put the card in my pocket. I don't know exactly what to say, so I simply thank him.

Boone leans in closer. "And by the way, I won't tell no one I'm Jet Brine's sponsor," he whispers. "I may be a southern boy, but I got cable TV down there, too, you know." He cracks a smile.

I chuckle nervously.

"Don't you fret it," he says, "I ain't no blabbermouth." He drapes an arm around me and walks with me to the door.

———

The same church basement, a different night, my turn to share. "Forty-one days away from the slots today," I proclaim proudly.

The attendees clap. Stan grins and nods.

Boone pumps a fist from across the circle. "Atta boy, atta slugger," he says, his beard bouncing.

———

"Fifty-five days without gambling." Excitement courses through me.

A wave of applause washes over the group.

I feel weightless. I'm actually participating in this thing called recovery, and I'm not failing at it.

"It's not all rainbows and butterflies, but I'm making it work," I say. "Some nights I hear the slots calling out for me. Thankfully, I have a good support system." I throw a smile at Boone.

---

The ovation dissolves over the group. Sixty-nine days without gambling is certainly worthy of applause, but I know what comes next. According to Boone and our GA literature, I need to make a list of all the people I've harmed with my gambling addiction, those whom I'm willing to make amends.

I cringe at the thought of the list, its length. But I do know where to begin: at the very top, the two people I hurt the most throughout the years.

I sit at the peeling wooden desk in my apartment to finally start the list. An old lamp shines down on my dog-eared paper. Janice leads off at number one. Jay is number two. Linda is batting third.

---

The thick clouds roil overhead, blotting out the sun. I hold the umbrella at my side, leaning on it. I place the flower bouquet on the moss before Janice's headstone. In the distance, the soothing hum of a lawnmower.

My bones ache as I utter her name. "Janny, babe," I say, "I'm sorry it's been so long." I glance around the graveyard quickly. "This place really needs your green thumb."

Raindrops start to fall. I open the umbrella. The mower comes to a stop in the background.

"I've been doing this Gamblers Anonymous thing," I say. "I think you'd be proud of me."

A memory of Janice holding up a GA pamphlet floods my mind like a tsunami. I see her well-meaning smile, but I laugh at her, waving her off with a dismissive hand.

"I'm so sorry, Janny." The rain increases and my feet sink further into the moss. "I'm sorry I did this to you." My tears blend with the rain. "I never meant to push you away..." I shudder. "Please forgive me."

I wait for a sign from her or from God, something to tell me I'm forgiven. I know God's doing something up there but a sign or some proof would be nice. The emerging, howling wind carries with it no such sign.

———————

My heart thumps hard against my chest.

I dial Jay's number from my kitchen.

I hear the dreaded out-of-service message.

I feel faint, like I'm about to be felled by the weight of Jay's silence. I grab for a nearby chair, its armrest. I climb into the chair, and for a moment I can hear his disappointed tone in my mind, like a whisper.

I want to apologize, to stare directly into his eyes and beg for his mercy, for his forgiveness. I shrink into the chair, shame racking my body.

Then, as suddenly as the shame arrived, my temples begin to throb with anger. And I want to replace the anger and shame with something as quickly as possible.

The bells and whistles of the jackpot fill my ears. I feel giddy, like I have a caffeine buzz. I fear what I might do, so I call Boone right away.

"Hey, slugger," he says. "Got the urge?"

I recount the situation with my son.

Boone reminds me about triggers, how all it takes is one trigger to send an addict back down the "dark road."

He clears his throat. "You're better than this, ain't you, slugger?"

Something about his voice calms me. "Yeah... I'm better than this."

# CHAPTER THIRTEEN

I CALL LINDA AND INVITE HER TO A MOVIE. I figure I need to make up for last time. I pick her up at her house. We take my car. I feel self-conscious about my vehicle as always. Rain taps on the windshield like fingers on a desk. I turn on the wipers. My wipers aren't smooth as they should be; they hesitate or sputter over the glass. The AC cools my knuckles on the steering wheel as Linda decides to speak from the passenger's seat.

"Mom asked about you the other day," she says randomly.

"Oh, yeah?"

"She asks about you all the time."

"What do you tell her?"

"Mostly, that you're a decent guy. That you're doing okay."

I turn to her briefly, thinking *a decent guy? Doing okay?* "You haven't told her about Gamblers Anonymous, right?"

"Of course not."

"Good, no one's supposed to know about that. It's anonymous."

She lets out what sounds like a forced chuckle. "I gathered that much."

"I wish I could give you details."

"I suppose as long as you're staying away, I don't need the details. I just want what's best for you." Her voice isn't tinged with happiness; it's devoid of any sort of tenderness or warmness.

Normally, she'd put her hand on my leg at this point, a comforting touch, but she keeps to herself. I wonder about that; she's kept to herself more than usual lately. I figure she must find the anonymity of my program bothersome, but she won't admit it for whatever reason.

In the theater, we join the long, snaking line. I salivate at the smell of fresh popcorn. We walk to the concessions after we retrieve our tickets.

"Wanna share a bag?" I ask to my side.

She shakes her head, eyes looking straight ahead. She avoids eye contact as we creep closer to the counter.

Inside the dim auditorium, we select our seats, a row to ourselves. I start munching on the popcorn. She sits in silence. The auditorium slowly fills.

"This is supposed to be really good," I whisper. "Got an eighty-five percent on Rotten Tomatoes."

Again, she keeps her eyes straight ahead. "Yeah, should be good," she says dryly.

The previews roll. I see her cross her arms out of the corner of my eye. *Maybe she's cold.* I'd offer her a jacket if I had one with me. Instead, I set my hand on her leg. She doesn't look down at it, doesn't join hands. Her eyes won't leave the screen. My hand sits there alone on an island.

"Is everything okay?" I whisper into her ear.

"It's fine. Let's just watch."

So, we watch as the previews eventually switch into the feature film. I remove my hand from her leg, and now I'm the one on an island. I glance over at her periodically; she never returns the glance.

I attempt to focus on the movie at hand. I must have missed part of the plot or something, because this movie makes absolutely no sense. *The butler killed who and why am I supposed to care? And who's this woman in the blue blouse? How does she play into this?*

I give up on the movie about twenty minutes in. I'm more interested in the drama to my right. I'm much more concerned about the fact that my girlfriend has barely looked into my eyes our last couple of visits and why, today, she won't hold my hand. *Did I say something wrong? Is she getting tired of me? Does she no longer find me attractive? Maybe that's it. She's finally gotten to know the real Jet Brine and she doesn't like what she sees.*

A spray of gunshots nearly knocks me out of my seat. My attention shoots up to the screen; the butler wields a pistol, a sinister smile widening on his face.

"That's what you get for sleeping with my wife," the butler says.

I look over to Linda, thinking, *Is there another guy? You wouldn't do that to me, would you? You're not that type of woman.* The thought of Linda kissing someone else causes me to feel queasy. I don't want to lose her. I can't lose her. She's the best thing in my life by far.

The end credits begin to roll. Linda doesn't waste any time; she stands and then starts toward the exit immediately. I follow suit, like a dog on a leash. I see her eyeing her cell as I trail her. She's texting someone but I can't make out the name. I finally catch up to her, walking side-by-side and an arm's length apart. She slips the cell back into her pocketbook.

Outside, with each step to the car, rain hits my head and face like rocks. She gallops ahead in her heels. I bolt to the car, my hands over my head, palms up to the sky, shielding myself from the pellets. I want to open the car door for her, but by the time I arrive at the car, she's already getting in. I run to the driver's side and jump in, my hands dripping.

Her phone buzzes. She goes fishing in her bag with a hand. The phone silences. She looks at me, finally she looks at me, and I expect to hear a kind, warm voice or something that resembles the Linda that I know, but she says, "I need to get home." That's all I get, a monotone, robotic voice telling me it's time to part ways.

I kick the car into reverse, my breath quickening, and I leave the parking lot thinking of a faceless guy on the other end of her phone. Some anonymous guy ready to take her away from me. My throat swells and I can't think of anything productive to say, so I just blurt, "Just tell me what's going on!"

She flinches.

"I mean," I say, dialing back a bit, "is everything okay? Like *really* okay?"

The rain continues beating down on the car, trying to break in.

"We definitely need to talk," she says.

Those five words cause my hands to tremble.
I've heard these words before and they rarely
lead to anything positive.

"Okay, let's talk," I say.

"Let's get back to my place and we'll talk."

She probably doesn't want to give me any
bad news while I'm driving, for fear of a car acci-
dent. She turns on the radio, talk radio, and we
listen to a political nut rave and rant about the
president—how he should do this and do that
and say this and say that. None of this matters
to me right now. I don't think any of it matters
to Linda, either. I guess she needs to fill the air
with some sound, any sound.

We enter her driveway, the rain waning.
"Come inside. I'll make coffee," she says, scanning the house.

We go inside. She directs me to the screened-
in patio. She flips on a light. I sit in one of her
straw chairs. She sits in a chair in front of me.
She stares into my eyes; it's not a warm gaze, and
her eyes certainly aren't sparkling. She looks

on me now as she would a regular Joe Schmoe co-worker or insubordinate.

"I've had a lot on my mind lately," she says softly. "I'm sure you can tell."

"Okay, so I haven't gone totally crazy, then."

"No," she says, her eyes downcast. "It's complicated, Jet. You have to believe me when I tell you it's complicated."

"I don't know what you're getting at, but okay."

She looks up at me. "Well, you've been doing all this great work for yourself. You seem to be doing pretty well. No gambling lately, correct?"

"Right."

She smiles, she finally smiles. "And, see, that's great," she says. "But I feel as though you still have a long way to go for yourself. I've been reading up on addiction and most of the books say the same thing..."

My heart sinks. "What do they say?" I know what they say, but I'm trying to play dumb, to stop the inevitable.

"They mostly say it's best for an addict to not be in a relationship during recovery." She pauses, then starts up again, "And there's so much I need to consider and ponder, and I want what's best for you, too—"

"Are you really trying to tell me what I think you're trying to tell me?"

"Again, it's complicated. More complicated than you know," she says with a sigh.

Tears begin to fall onto my fractured chest. "But this is good. We have a good thing going here," I say, pleading my case. "You can't just walk away now... when I'm so close..."

"Jet," she says firmly, "I want you to keep working on yourself, keep going to your meetings. I want you to soar." She swallows her tears. "I want you to keep swinging... Swing as hard as you can." She breaks down, her hands covering her eyes, sobbing.

I want to console her. I'm the one with the smashed heart, but I want to console her. It seems backwards, but I walk over to her. She stands and we hug. Her tears soak my shoulder.

"Tell me you'll keep swinging, okay?" she sniffles. She squeezes a little more tightly, like she's trying to force a reply. "Tell me."

"I will," I breathe. But, truthfully, I'm unsure if I can keep doing anything at all, let alone swinging at life's opportunities.

She releases me from the hug.

"I have to ask," I say, "is there someone else?" I flinch at my own inquiry. I'm not sure if I want to hear her answer. I won't be able to handle thinking of her with Faceless Joe.

She doesn't avoid eye contact. Her eyes darken with concern. "There's no one else, Jet," she assures me. She wipes her face with a sleeve. "It's not like that. I'm not like that. You have to trust me."

I'm not sure that I trust her, but I feel compelled to leave before I completely lose it. I need some consoling. I need someone to lean on, someone to hold and cry on. *What about me? Don't I count?*

"I'm gonna go now," I say finally.

She grimaces, then gives a slow nod. I turn around, leaving her behind on the patio. I walk through the living room. The urn, my signed baseball card on the mantel, they catch my eye. I feel the urge to break down, to absolutely and totally break down and crumble to my knees right here in this room. I somehow will myself out of the room, out the front door, out of her life.

In the car, I dial Boone's number.

It rings numerous times.

He doesn't pick up.

I call again.

And again.

And again.

"Hey, slugger," he answers. "You ain't back-slidin', are ya?"

"Not yet, but I want to."

"There ain't gonna be no relapsin' for you. You're—"

"I'm dying." I pause. "I'm dying inside," I clarify.

"Don't do nothin' rash. Let's meet up."

"Are you sure? It's really late."

"This is what I do," he says. "You know that diner on Ansel Lane? The one that looks like it's stuck in the fifties."

"Yeah."

"I'll be there in ten."

I agree to meet him at the diner instead of racing to the casino to wash the pain away. He's no Janice or Linda, that's for sure but, as the song says, everyone needs someone to lean on. But most importantly, I need someone to see me, to truly see me and to acknowledge that yes, I do count.

# CHAPTER FOURTEEN

"Peggy, your turn—would you like to share anything today?" Holly rests her hands on her head-honcho table. Her gaze sweeps over the sales team—*her* sales team—in this upstairs conference room. We sit in a half-circle in front of her.

Peggy, from her spot out here among the peons, starts in with her squealing voice, "I was speaking to Andy from the shop the other day and he asked if I could remind everyone to please wear their safety glasses when entering the shop floor." Peggy sits back in her chair, her proud chin lifted. She begins tapping on the table with her pen.

From across the room, I notice Fred's eyes fall into the back of his head with disgust. Another co-worker, Emily, does the same. Everyone knows Peggy is very popular with the male workers in the shop. She's practically their unofficial spokesperson.

"And you, Fred?" Holly's eyes bore into him; I think she noticed his upturned eyes, too. "Would you like to share?" Her verbiage reminds me of Gamblers Anonymous.

"Umm," he hesitates, "not today, thanks." He tugs at his large earlobe, his face reddening.

"And Emily?" Holly asks, working her way through the team.

Red-haired Emily opens her notepad. She flips through the pages, then points to a page. "Ah, yes, that's right," she says, sounding rehearsed, "as a reminder, we have our family outing on Friday during lunch break. A picnic lunch will be provided and will be held outside the cafeteria on the back lawn."

Holly expounds upon the message, "And, of course, feel free to bring your family—you know, the wife, the kids. Your call. It will be a fun time for all."

I sink into my hard chair. *A family picnic? Really? Who can I bring?*

"It will be a wonderful opportunity to mingle and get to know one another on a deeper level," Holly carries on. "Team-building at its best."

I picture myself sitting alone during the picnic, my—

"Jet, is there anything you'd like to include today?" Holly interrupts my train of thought.

I never truly have anything to add during these meetings, and especially now—after the heart-shattering bomb Linda dropped on me—I'm more indifferent about this setup than ever before. So, I simply shake my head, then say, "Nothing to share today, thanks."

With a clap of her hands, she says, "All right, well, back to work." She stands. "We have lots of rush orders in need of attention today and lots of prospects ready to be sold."

The team stands in unison, except for me. I move a little slower these days in everything that I do. The team leaves the room single file. I trail behind them, heavy-footed and heart sagging.

*What should I do if I see Linda at the picnic? Will she even be there?* I run through several scenarios in my mind, the first being the most obvious: She spots me from a distance, chooses to sit somewhere else, with her mother perhaps—or another man. *The* other man.

My stomach plummets as I ponder this terrible scenario.

Then my thoughts fall on Jay, and how nice it would be to have him around to call my son. I crave normal fatherhood in moments like these. A normal father-son relationship would certainly include a hug as he arrives at the picnic. It would include proudly introducing my strapping son to my co-workers. Then Jay and I could play a game of catch and show off our arms to everyone watching...

If a heart can sigh, mine's sighing now.

---

A hand drops a rush purchase order into my bin.

Another hand throws an order on top of that one.

By eleven, my bin overflows with orders. I can't keep up, nor do I have a desire to do so. I consider removing a couple orders from the bin and tossing them in the garbage or the shredder near the copy machine. *Would anyone notice?*

Peggy's music kicks on and I'm reminded of my neighbors on either side of me. On cue, the egg smell wafts in my direction from Fred's cubicle. *Surely, he'd notice if I threw away orders. He seems to notice everything. He's got this place bugged.*

I squint at the computer screen, the hourglass spinning as the machine thinks. The computer fan grows louder. The hourglass keeps whirling and whirling, like the invisible hourglass of my life. Ever since Linda broke up with me, my life has stood still, frozen as this computer. Time keeps moving around me, yes, but just barely. I'm stuck in this same lethargic mode every day. Funny, I guess—or kind of ironic—considering my name is Jet.

---

The night before the family picnic, I call Boone.

I don't know if it's outside the rules of the group to invite him to a work-related event, or to spend time together at a non-group-related function, but I invite him to the picnic anyway. He's not family, per se, but no one needs to know that.

I hear him smile over the phone. "Slugger, I'll be there," he says. "Just do me a favor, don't sit me near the Egg Man. I reckon I'd have to leave right quick." He chuckles. He's heard about my coworkers more than I'd like to admit.

"Oh, don't you worry. We'll be staying as far away from him as possible."

———————

Friday rears its head at last. Warm air blows through the fresh-cut lawn teeming with smiling parents and children on picnic tables. A banner hangs over a tent by the building that reads **16th ANNUAL FAMILY OUTING.**

Boone and I step into the dwindling line beside a buffet-style table.

He leans in close to me and whispers, "You see her yet?" He adds a sub roll to his paper plate.

I give him a look that says to shut up.

"I'm just curious," he counters, but he really means, "What's the big deal for asking?" He stabs at a slice of ham with a plastic fork.

I create my sandwich as well, stomach rumbling due to nerves, not hunger. Truth be told, my appetite is severely lagging lately.

We sit at a picnic table together, just the two of us. Now that we're alone, I say, "She's not here. I don't see her anywhere."

In between bites, he says, "Are you sure?"

I scan the lawn once more. "Yeah, she must be traveling. Or she stayed home."

"She don't dare, if you ask me. She don't dare show up here after the way she treated you."

I shrug, but he might be right.

Peggy suddenly appears at our table. She extends a hand to Boone. "And you must be—"

"This is Boone," I answer for him, trying to take control of the conversation early. "Peggy, Boone. Boone, Peggy."

His eyes widen at me as if to inquire, "*The* Peggy?"

"Are you Jet's brother?" she asks.

"Somethin' like that," he chuckles. "Brother from a different momma."

The joke obviously falls flat on her. "Oh, you're Jet's half-brother, then?"

Boone's eyes dart over to me, like "Is this broad for real?" Boon laughs—one of those deep belly laughs. I join along. Peggy merely blinks at us, confusion flooding her face.

"Hello, everyone... I want to thank you for joining us here on this beautiful day," a man's voice sounds through a bullhorn. Everyone pauses their conversations, looks to him. I think he's one of the higher-ups, a VP of something. He's wearing a loose tie over an untucked dress shirt; his attempt of appearing playful or casual, I suppose.

"As a family-focused company, I can proudly say that we've held one of these get-togethers each year since our inception." He briefly inspects the crowd. "I see a lot of new faces here today and some old faces."

"Hey!" a lady yells out jokingly from a far-off table.

"Okay, *familiar* faces," the man laughs. "Seriously, though, it's great to see all the families as always. I'm sure you'll agree that this is what life is truly about... Again, thanks for coming and bringing your families. Cheers!"

I return my attention to Boone. Peggy has turned her back to us; she's walking back to her table.

"I know what you're thinkin'," Boone says, "and it ain't true."

"What am I thinking?"

"That your family ain't here."

"But they're not."

"Family ain't always blood." Boone smiles.

———

"I'm sure you realize why I called you in here again today," Holly says. She pulls out a folder from her desk drawer.

"Not really, sorry," I say, but I think I know.

She opens the folder and shuffles through the pages. "I'm sure you're aware that as an employee with a formal warning on file, the ice is very thin for you."

I don't try to defend myself at this point. I'm aware that I haven't been doing my best lately. I know what's coming. . .

"Unfortunately, we've noticed a sharp decline in your work performance as of late, and after much deliberation, we've decided to terminate your employment effective immediately."

*I guess Linda's done vouching for me these days.*

Holly stands. "I'll need you to hand over your badge." She extends an open-palmed hand to me. "Security will see you out," she says, absent of any emotion.

The door opens. A man in a black suit darkens the doorway. Death has arrived. He's just missing a hood and a scythe.

On the way out, I feel eyes on me, stinging me all over.

"Oh, my," Peggy squeals as I walk by her music-blaring cubicle.

I catch one last whiff of Fred. I look back at him, his egg salad sandwich in a baggy next to his mousepad.

---

It's 2:11 a.m. and I can't sleep.

The AC in my apartment rattles overhead.

Muffled voices speak through the walls.

The bathroom faucet drips.

I turn on my bedside lamp and sit up. I need to get out of the house. I need to get in my car and just drive. Drive somewhere where something makes sense. Anything at all. I could drive to the 7-Eleven store down the road to get a snack and fill up my gas tank; it's nearly empty. A stomach needs food and a car needs gas. Makes sense. Anything to distract me from the ongoing insomnia and shut off my whirring mind. I think about giving Boone a call, but it's too late for that.

I throw on sweatpants and a white t-shirt. I climb into my car and take off toward the convenience store. I have every intention of going to the store, I honestly do, but along the way I spot those haunting, blinking lights. I'm drawn to the sign like a moth to a lightbulb.

The only car on the road, I put on my blinker. I gaze at the sign adoringly. Warmth fills my chest. *The slots make sense. Too much sense.* I want to turn back but I can't. The desire is too strong.

I reach for my cell. I should give Boone a call, my brother from a different momma, but that sign keeps blinking. If it had a voice, it would say, "Come inside." I know better than to listen. I just don't care.

I turn into the parking lot, my hands trembling on the steering wheel.

# CHAPTER FIFTEEN

"SLUGGER, YOU OKAY?" Boone's voice floats through the phone.

"No... I did it again. I was driving by and I couldn't resist. I went in and lost thousands. *Thousands.*"

"Where you at right now?"

"In the parking lot, in my car. I need to go back in and win my money back. I need to give it another shot."

"It ain't about the outcome, you reckon?" Boone repeats Stan's wisdom. "It ain't about the outcome, you gotta get that now."

"Well, I already messed up. Might as well see if I can dig myself out of this hole."

"Slugger, that ain't no way to dig out of a hole." I can hear frustration in his voice. "The hole's only gonna get bigger," he says.

"I... I don't know what to do."

"You gotta pull yourself up by the bootstraps and keep on pluggin' away... This ain't you, slugger. This is your condition talkin'."

"I know, I know... I need to keep swinging."

Then he begins to tell me about his first relapse. "I was thirty-six goin' on ten. I was supposed to be watchin' the kids that night, but I got the hankerin' for some cards. Lil' Clint was six and Sherry was eight. I reckon you know what happened next."

"You chose the cards over the kids, didn't you?"

"I chose cards over kids all too much. I never won no daddy of the year awards, that's for sure. And I still ain't winnin' awards."

"Yeah, me neither," I scoff at myself.

"Gretchen gave me my walkin' papers the next week." His tone turns somber. "I reckon she wasn't too happy when she came home from workin' and found the kiddos alone, fendin' for themselves."

I cringe at the thought, realizing that I wasn't any better as a father.

"You turn those keys and start that car of yours, ya hear?" Boone says. "Drive the heck outta there like a bat outta hell. Never look back."

Reality rushes over me. Shame twists at my stomach. I turn the key in the ignition, hear the car purr—*no*, roar—and I peel out of the dimly-lit parking lot.

"All right, I'm gone," I tell Boone over the speakerphone. "I'm going back home."

"Atta boy, slugger." Boone shares his approval. "What you doin' out so late, anyhow? How'd you get into this mess?"

I explain how I couldn't sleep, that I innocently thought going for a ride would be okay, that I had forgotten the casino was on the way to 7-Eleven.

"I've gone down that road before but I forgot," I say. "Conveniently, I guess."

"Yeah, you've gone down that road one too many times. I reckon it's time to find a new road, whatcha think?"

"I'll take a different road from now on."

———————

Money is dwindling once again, but I refuse to return to the casino, so I decide that I should set up shop at one of the larger memorabilia conventions. I thought I was done with these; however, I need to eat and pay the bills. I get out of the car, my shirt sticking to my back in the summer heat. I scoop up my worn duffle bag from the backseat.

On the way to the entrance, I cross paths with box-wielding dealers. Their eyes dart to me, sizing me up. I scoot through the double doors of the building. I locate the event manager and he shows me to my two tables. I methodically lay out the 8x10's and the bobbleheads. I put all my rookie cards in two stacks side-by-side. I place a sticker on the top of each stack indicating **$5 EACH OR 2 FOR $8**. I figure if I sell both stacks, that money will go toward groceries this week.

Then I place all the bat and jersey cards in their own piles. The bat cards are some of my favorites. They each include an embedded piece of a game-used bat. The jersey cards follow the same marketing strategy—pieces of my game-used jerseys have been implanted in the cards. These memorabilia cards book for at least $10 each, but I place a sticker on them for **$8 EACH OR 2 FOR $14**. I might even surprise the buyers and sign a few of them as a bonus.

A crowd slowly converges on the convention center, on the tables. The usual dickering takes place.

"I'll give you five dollars," one man says, pointing to a jersey card.

"How 'bout six bucks for this one," another voice spouts.

I agree to all the haggling, sign a few autographs, and shake a few hands. Of course, the occasional passerby mutters words about the blown World Series. Thankfully, none of those people decide to stop by my tables.

One of my dealer neighbors chows down on an egg and cheese sandwich during lunch and I can't help but think of Fred from the office. This guy bears no resemblance to Fred physically, but the familiar scent causes me to recoil slightly. I packed a peanut butter and jelly sandwich, but I've lost my appetite.

At one o'clock, another wave of potential customers attacks my table. A couple small hands rifle through the stacks of cards. The little hands leave the cards scattered over the table. I gather them together and put them back into neat stacks. Then a grandmother and her grandson come to the table.

"I want that one!" The boy points to one of my bat cards.

His grandmother pulls out a wad of money and hands me a ten-dollar bill.

I lean in to the boy. "Would you like me to sign it for you?"

His face brightens. He nods.

I sign the card in sharpie marker just over the bat. I hand it to him and he turns a deeper shade of red.

"Awesome!" He shows the card to his grandmother.

The hands on the wall clock remind me of the office—slow motion is the clock's default speed. *But I guess this is better than entering orders.* It definitely beats a prattling Peggy and a boss breathing down my neck.

At two o'clock, a man speaks from a microphone on the stage.

"Come on up and get your raffle tickets," he says. "Winner gets to take part in a meet-and-greet with baseball great Aaron Love. You'll also receive a signed baseball."

I look down my table, to the three signed baseballs in ball protector cases. For some reason, no one has ever bought any of my signed baseballs. I pick one up and inspect the sticker. I have it listed for fifty dollars. I pull out another sticker and scribble **$35 SALE!** on it. I replace the original sticker with this sale sticker. *It's worth a try.*

Four o'clock slowly emerges. I check my wallet, count through the money. I've made two hundred twenty-five dollars on the day. *There's gotta be more.* I count again. *Nope, that's the right amount.*

More hands hover over my table. They scatter my cards and photos and disappear out of view. At one point, I hear a man's southern voice, thinking of Boone. I look up; it's not him.

A voice blares over the speaker system announcing the winner of the raffle. A wobbling old man leaning on a cane raises his hand, "I won! I won!" He's acting like he just won the lottery. *Or the jackpot in a casino game.*

The desire strikes my veins like lightning. *I could make so much more money at the slots. And I wouldn't have to lug around all this crap and do all the setup and listen to fanboys drone on and on.* I quickly withdraw from my thoughts, shaking them off. *I can't go down that road.*

Another hand reaches over the table—a soft, feminine hand holding a rolled-up event program. I follow the hand up the arm, to the chest, to the face of a smiling Linda. My heart dances but I can only give a partial smile. She unrolls the program and points to my picture.

"Says here Jet Brine will be offering his personal collection of memorabilia and will be signing autographs," she says. She looks into my eyes.

"Would you like an autograph?" I ask jokingly.

"How about this one?" She seizes the signed baseball. "Oh, and it's on sale."

She reaches into her purse.

"You don't need to do that," I say.

"Come on, let me—"

"No, seriously, you don't need to do that. I don't need a handout."

Her eyes roll to the ceiling. "I'm sorry, Jet. I'm so sorry," she says, her face serious. She returns the baseball.

"What are you really doing here, Linda?"

"I wanted to see you. I wanted to speak with you."

"I can't erase what you said before about—"

A potential customer appears behind Linda in a Red Sox shirt, so I pause. Oblivious, the customer man steps in front of Linda and reaches out his hand.

"I can't believe it's you," he says. "*The* Jet Brine."

I watch as Linda moves off to the side. I want to push this guy out of the way, to tell him that we were in the middle of a conversation, that he should come back later and he's being rude, but he starts in again, "I was there at that World Series game."

I work hard to refrain from rolling my eyes. *Oh, here we go again.*

"You're probably one of the most polarizing guys in baseball," he continues. "Me personally, I think you should be inducted into the Hall."

I take a step back, unsure of how to respond.

"Everyone talks about that last at bat but no one mentions the most obvious. If it weren't for you the Sox wouldn't have been in the World Series that year to begin with." The man's eyes begin to sparkle. "Your homer in game six of the ALCS saved the season for us that year."

I feel Linda's warmth. I glance at her; she's beaming.

The man picks up the remaining cards on the table, balancing the stacks in his arms. "How much for the lot?" he asks.

I think for a moment. "Hundred bucks," I say finally.

He sets down a stack and pulls out a Benjamin, trembling. "What a deal!"

"Do you want me to sign any of them?"

He translates that as, "Do you want me to sign *all* of them?"

He hands the cards to me, one by one, and I sign each one, smiling. Then he asks if he can get a picture of the two of us. Linda is still smiling.

"My son isn't going to believe this!" he snaps the selfie of the two of us.

He shakes my hand one final time and steps away, blending with the circling crowd.

Linda steps up to the table. "It's nice to see you getting some deserved praise for once," she says.

"I agree. It's few and far between."

"Again, I'm sorry about what happened to us—and to you at the office," she says as she places a hand on mine.

I stare at the hand, wondering if I should pull away, if I should retreat from this conversation altogether.

"Can we have a talk?" she asks.

I hesitate but nod. "I pack up at six."

# CHAPTER SIXTEEN

WE DRIVE IN OUR SEPARATE VEHICLES toward a state park beach about ten miles from the convention center. I follow her luxury car through the winding roads to a manned booth at the park's gate. I roll down my window at the booth. A sign indicates a ten-dollar entry fee. I pull a bill from my wallet.

"You're all set," the booth attendant says, waving me onward.

Linda, from her car in front of mine, puts a hand up to direct me forward as well.

I let out a laugh. *Of course, she took care of it.* I return the bill to its leathery home and roll into the park. I find a parking spot beside her car and we both exit our cars at nearly the same moment. I watch in silence as she pops her trunk. She rummages around in the trunk for a moment, then pulls out a pair of black Teva sandals. She slips into them and tosses her heels into the car.

"Are you okay in those?" she asks, glancing at my sneakers.

"I'll take them off on the beach."

We lock our cars and start on toward the outstretched sand.

"Thanks for agreeing to this," she says in her corporate voice.

I nod, and kneel on the warm sand. I remove my socks and sneakers, and put them aside. We continue our evening walk, the balmy air blowing through us, our feet kicking up sand with each step. In the distance, out at sea, waves crash and echo over the beach like an applause from a stadium crowd.

"I had to see you, Jet," she says, her hands swinging by her sides. "I've missed you."

I look over at her as we walk, an orange tinge from the setting sun glowing on her hair and face. "I'm not gonna lie. You really hurt me," I say. "Losing you was like losing a piece to a much larger puzzle, and now I can't finish it. It just sits there collecting dust with that one piece missing."

She draws in a long breath, pushes it out. "I'm so sorry I hurt you," she says, pain present in her voice.

We stop at a rocky spot on the beach. We climb atop the rocks and sit opposite one another. We watch as the sun starts to dip below the horizon, painting the sky with long brush strokes of color.

"I've felt such utter emptiness since that day, Jet." Her eyes turn downward to the rocks. "It sounds terrible, but I tried to shake you off. I tried to move on. I didn't want to complicate your life for the sake of your recovery... and—"

"I'm sorry but I just can't believe that it had anything to do with my recovery," I say abruptly. "Come on, you said so yourself that things are complicated in your life."

"They are. And it's true about the recovery. It's what I've read in—"

"So, what's changed?"

Her brow knots in thought. "I suppose if I have to put it into words, I discovered that you're my missing puzzle piece, too," she says, locking eyes with me. "I need to have you in my life in some way, complications or not. I don't know how any of that actually looks, though, or how it can work."

"I honestly don't care what they say about being in a relationship during recovery," I blurt. "I'm doing just fine. I don't need anyone else calling the shots in that regard." I think of my recent relapse, how I'm barely *just fine,* but she doesn't need to know about that situation.

"Perhaps each person's different when it comes to recovery, I don't know," she says. "I don't want to stand in your way, but I don't want to lose you completely, either."

"And I don't want to lose you."

"Can we agree to stay in touch?" she asks, her eyes hopeful.

"Is this you saying that you want to be just friends?"

"I don't know what it means, exactly. I simply—"

"Please tell me I'm not some plan B you want to keep around in case something else doesn't work out."

"No, it's definitely not like that at all," she says with restrained horror. "I'm confused. Everyone looks to me to have all the answers, but I'm the confused one now. The only thing I know for certain is that I want—*need*—you in my life."

"I don't know if I can just be friends. I don't know if I can do that to myself." I pause for a moment, then, "but I want you in my life. *Need* you in my life." My heart pounds in my throat at that.

"Well, then, let's not put a label on it," she proposes. "Why does everyone always have to label everything in life? We have labels for everything and everyone. Why can't we just *be?*"

"Are you sure there isn't another guy?"

Her look of horror returns. "I'll say it again. There's no one else. I promise you."

I desperately want to believe her. "I guess I can just be. If that means that I can have you around."

She smiles. "Thank you." She stands from the rock. She touches the top of my hand briefly.

I follow suit by standing. We turn and walk to the water. She steps in with her sandals and I with my bare feet. We stand in the lukewarm water, the distant waves pushing the water up to our ankles. I reach out for her hand, but her hand remains by her side, her gaze fastened on the painted sky. *Maybe she didn't notice my hand*, I think to myself.

"Do you ever wonder how the sky can be all these colors, all at once?" She remains transfixed by the sky.

I don't know the answer, plus I think it's a rhetorical question anyway. "It *is* beautiful," I reply.

"You know, when I was a little girl, I used to come to this beach with Dad," she says, her eyes moving over the heavens. "Every once in a while, he'd take me here, just the two of us, and we'd dance in the sun and play some ball and build sand castles." Her eyes come back down to earth, to me. "And on some nights, he'd carry his telescope onto the beach." She points at the rocks where we sat. "He'd set up over there," she says, pointing to another rocky formation, "or over there." She pauses as her eyes glisten. "He'd say, 'Linny, *look*, that's Orion's Belt,' or 'Linny, it's the North Star,' and I couldn't believe how much knowledge he had."

I scarcely remember my father, never mind being able to share a story like hers. I feel a fleeting bit of jealousy, and a stab of pain or sadness that Jay would probably feel the same about me, but I quickly snap out of that state of mind as she says, "Dad used to tell me that the stars put things into perspective. He said, 'Linny, no matter what you're going through in life, no matter how hard life gets, the stars are a reminder that God's at work all around us.'" She looks at me, her eyes hazy. "I find solace in that to this day," she adds. "Life may be complicated and confusing but there's someone bigger than us at work."

Water laps at my feet. "I think I believe that," I say, thinking of signs from God and wanting to see them clearly, especially if they pertain to Janice and her forgiveness. I reach out my hand once again. She takes hold of it this time. I'm unsure what this means for us, whether we're headed for another relationship, or if she's just vulnerable after speaking of her father. But we agreed to avoid the labels for now.

She turns and wraps her arms around me, hugging me tight. Then her embrace loosens and she rests her head on my shoulder. Neither one of us says anything for several minutes.

The sun finally disappears beneath the horizon. The stars slowly begin to dot the darkening sky. The moon peeks through the disappearing clouds. I wonder if Linda can hear her father's voice echoing somewhere in between the sounds of the waves.

She lifts her head from my shoulder. "Look, Jet, it's the North Star," she says, gazing up at the sky like a child.

I stare at the sky, squinting. She points at the star. "Right there," she says, jumping.

The star flickers back at us as if to say hello. I've seldom had this feeling in my life, the feeling of being in the right place at the right time, the feeling of belonging. *Simply belonging.* But right now, at this single moment, beneath a sea of stars shining millions of miles away, I feel like I belong.

"Your dad was right," I say.

"Oh?"

"Life may be complicated and confusing," I repeat, "but God's at work all around us."

She grins at me. The grin exudes the warmth I expect from her, the warmth that disappeared unexpectedly a while back. Here we stand, without labels, just being. I want to just be, I really do, but I think I'll always want more from her.

I want to lean in and kiss her, to feel her smooth lips on mine, to feel the surge of energy course through my body. I wish I could scoop her up into my arms and carry her back to the car. We could drive back to her house and touch and caress and disappear into one another.

But, for now, this will have to do.

She rests her head on my shoulder once again, her eyes aimed at the speckled sky. "Can we stay here a while longer?" she asks.

"Of course."

Truthfully, I wish I could stay here with her forever. There's something about her warmth that fills my emptiness. The warmth finds those cavernous crevices inside me and flows through them like water.

But, mostly, I'm just glad my missing puzzle piece has returned.

# CHAPTER SEVENTEEN

**I SIT IN MY CUSTOMARY CHAIR IN GROUP.** Boone fills the seat next to mine. I notice a few new faces in the circle as the sharing begins.

Stan makes his way to me, but first he points to the familiar woman with the ponytail, Natalie. She's attended every one of my group sessions. As expected, she slouches in his chair.

"I got into some trouble with a loan shark," she admits, her eyes aimed at the floor. "I had been over a month clean and I slipped up. I had to sell my car to pay back the loan." She gives a couple deep sighs. "So, no car for me at the moment. Thankfully, my friend offered to drive me around."

Stan cringes but replies with kindness, "Remember, recovery is a marathon, not a sprint.

Relapses happen but you need to brush your-self off and get back on track."

I glance at Boone. He nods at me.

Stan calls on the man with the black hat. I've learned his name is Derrick. He speaks proudly for once, like he's been waiting for the opportunity to speak: "I haven't pawned anything to fund my addiction for months. And I've kept myself away from the track."

"Atta boy," Boone blurts from my side, and he starts the applause with a slow clap. The group follows his lead, and soon, the clapping floods the room. I look to Boone because I see a pause in him out of the corner of my eye; he stopped clapping mid-clap, his face suddenly like the color of ash.

Stan calls my name to share.

My eyes remain affixed on Boone. Now sweat beads on his forehead and his breathing turns to loud panting.

"Boone, are you all right?" Stan finally takes notice.

Boone waves us on, but then he hunches forward and begins to clutch at his chest. His animal-like panting morphs into loud wheezing sounds.

I turn in my seat and grab him before he tumbles to the stained carpet.

"Someone call 9-1-1!" I thunder. I pull Boone into the upright position as he continues holding the middle of his chest.

He cries out like a wounded animal, "Get me... to a... hospital. *Get me there!*"

I look over at Stan and his ear is already pressed against his cell. He quickly explains the emergency. I give the room a scan. Some in the group display their nerves by rocking back and forth in their seats; pacing around the room; or biting their nails. Derrick joins me at Boone's side.

Boone howls, "When they comin'? When they... gonna be here?"

Stan turns his head away from the phone. "They're on their way!" he shouts. "Five minutes." He stays on the line.

When the paramedics finally arrive, they strap him into a stretcher and cart him away in a flurry of noise and movements. I trail behind them, intently watching as they lift my brother into the ambulance.

"Can I go with him?" I ask one of the paramedics.

"Are you family?"

I ponder the question for a moment, then, "Yes."

He motions me into the truck with another paramedic. I sit behind Boone's stretcher, his body convulsing. A hand slams the truck's door shut and we start moving. They quickly hook him up to portable machines and place a respirator mask on his face, all the while spouting technical terms to one another in what seems like a foreign language.

They hurriedly stick him with a needle and his shuddering stops moments later. His eyes slowly roll back in his head and his eyes flutter shut. He issues a sound of gargling. I reach over to him to touch his head, to touch something or anything to console him, but a paramedic brushes my hand away and gives me a quick stare as if to say, "Lay off."

My breathing hurries. "You're gonna be all right, Boone!" I shout. "You'll be okay, you hear me? I'm right here!"

At the hospital, men and women in scrubs roll him away down a busy corridor and out of sight. I consider following them down the hallway but a nurse tugs at my arm.

"He's in good hands," she says. Then she guides me to the waiting area. As she turns her heel to walk in the opposite direction, she says, "We'll keep you updated as we're able."

I pace around the room, unable to sit. The thought of losing Boone causes my breathing to hurry once again. *Calm down, Jet. It will be okay.*

I walk by the glassed-in vestibule and I notice Stan from group approaching the automatic doors in a panic.

He steps through the entrance. "Is he okay?" he asks me, his voice frantic. "Where is he?"

I point to the corridor. "They're... working on him." My voice cracks. "They said they'd keep me posted."

Then Derrick from group walks into the waiting room, followed by Natalie, her ponytail swaying as she walks. They each ask for an update and ask for Boone's whereabouts. This time, before I can speak, Stan points to the corridor and tells them we are waiting for word from the doctors.

I eventually wind up in a seat out of pure exhaustion, my face in my sweaty palms. I look up from my hands periodically, hoping to see an approaching doctor or nurse. A couple of nurses scurry by the room at one point, but neither of them stops to provide any information. The group members and I share nervous looks from our seats.

Derrick gradually falls asleep in his chair. His arm dangles off to the side. Natalie passes the time by listening to music in her headphones. She stares blankly at a far wall, slumped in her chair as always.

Every sound from the intercom and every step of passersby sends my heart down to my toes in fear. I want an update, but I fear an update. I cling to the adage that no news is good news.

Hours pass.

Then, without notice, the same nurse who showed me the waiting room steps before me. I figure it's a positive sign that they didn't send a doctor. A doctor in this case could mean death. They wouldn't send a nurse to the waiting area to inform loved ones of a death.

"You can come with me if you'd like to see him," she says.

I stand. The group members sit upright, even Derrick's alert now. Natalie removes her headphones.

The nurse looks to them. "Family only at this stage," she says in a forced tone of kindness.

They give me puzzled stares, but I continue with the nurse out of the room, down the corridor. She leaves me at room 356. I step through the doorway.

"Slugger..." Boone's groggy voice calls out.

I sit in a chair at his bedside. I notice the tubes in his nose and a monitor beeping near a wall, reminding me of Janice, my sweet Janny.

"I ain't... doin' so good," Boone says. "They got me," breathing heavily, "all hopped up." He points to the IV stuck in his arm. "They ran the EKG and they reckon I had a heart attack. A *big* one. They gonna keep me here a while for observin'."

"It looks like they have it under control now," I say, attempting to comfort him.

"Never had a brother." He breathes. "I... always wanted one but—"

"Brother from another momma," I say, working to smile. "That's me."

He lets out a laugh, causing him to go into a coughing fit.

"Are you okay?" I put a hand on his blanketed leg.

He clears his throat loudly, like a cat coughing up a fur ball. His breathing becomes steady.

"Not what we had in mind... for group today," he says, his tone unsteady.

"Is this your way of getting me out of sharing today?"

A sardonic smile stretches over his face. "You got me—"

One of the machines emits a string of loud, uneven beeps. We both look over to the machine. Neither of us knows what that indicates. I fully expect a doctor or a nurse to rush into the room, but no one appears. Either they have forgotten about us or the sound is normal.

"I wish Clint and Sherry could be here." His voice grows sentimental.

I recall the names of his children from a previous conversation. I imagine myself in a hospital bed. I wonder how Jay would react, if he'd come by to support his father. *How would he find out, anyway?*

Boone's eyelids droop, sadness seemingly overcoming him. "Truth be told, they wouldn't be caught dead here by my side." He blinks out a tear. "I ain't no daddy of the year, but I don't deserve this. Ain't I a good man now?" His wheezing returns.

"You're a good man..." I touch his hand. "But you're getting yourself worked up. *Breathe...*"

He takes, it seems, a calculated breath. "Slugger... promise me somethin'." He turns his head on the pillow, looking up at the popcorn ceiling, pondering something.

"What is it?"

"Promise me you won't go relapsin' again." His request splits the air like an ax. "Promise me you'll keep goin' down the different road."

"I don't know if I can promise that sort of thing."

He turns his head to me. He eyes me, awaiting a different response. "You promise me you ain't gonna go relapsin', okay? You just promise."

I can't figure out why this is so important to him right here and now. But I can't keep denying a man in a hospital bed. Can't keep denying my brother.

"I promise." I push the words out, knowing that I can't take them back.

He smiles. Footsteps somewhere behind me catch his attention. I think of doctors or nurses.

"Gretchen," he says, looking beyond me. "What are ya doin' here?"

"I'm still your emergency contact," she says. "After all these years, you apparently kept me on the list..." She steps through the doorway toward the bed.

"Was itchin' to see ya." He winks.

This is my cue to leave the room and I know it. I lean in and hug him. "See you soon, slugger," he whispers.

I nod at Gretchen as I scoot past her.

"Who was that?" she asks, and she shuts the door behind me.

I stand in the hallway and watch them for a moment through the door window. I can't make out the words. She waves her hands in the air and he laughs at her. His kids aren't here, but at least his ex-wife showed up. *That should count for something.*

I turn a heavy heel and start down the corridor. I pass by a couple of doctors holding clipboards, and some nurses having a lively discussion about the patient in room 322. I arrive in the waiting room. Natalie is gone, but Derrick and Stan remain.

Stan stands from his seat. "So, how is he?"

"They confirmed it was a heart attack," I say. "He's on a lot of meds and they have him on monitors. But he's lucid and seems better."

He lets out a sigh of relief. "Maybe it looked worse than it is."

"I hope so."

"Glad he's recovering," says Derrick, leaning in from his chair.

Stan and I sit together. He asks if I'm hungry. I tell him I don't have much of an appetite. Derrick says he could eat something small, a snack. The two agree to visit the hospital cafeteria together or the vending machines.

"I'll be here," I say as they disappear down the hallway. I'll be here until I see Gretchen cross through the waiting area, then I'll check his room for another update. *She's probably just stopping by. She'll be gone in an hour.*

Ten minutes pass. Fifteen. Twenty. Twenty-five. *What, did they get lost? Decide to eat a four-course meal?*

Then, to my surprise, Gretchen appears from out of the corridor, her eyes bleary, her hands trembling. She steps to me. "Jet... right?"

Horror grows in my stomach, the type of horror that one can't define. *They got into a fight, that's all. Just a simple fight. She's his ex. Makes sense.*

"They're in there now," she says, her voice wobbly. "They're taking him away."

*"What?"* I just saw him. He was cracking jokes and smiling. He was right there in that bed calling me slugger and giving advice.

She swallows hard. "He's gone."

This doesn't add up. Can't be true. "Where are they taking him?"

"He flatlined." She avoids eye contact, tears streaming down her face.

I grab onto the back of a nearby chair, holding myself up. Derrick and Stan appear behind Gretchen. Their eyes grow round at the sight of us. Gretchen takes a quick step forward and wraps her arms around me. She buries her head into my shattered chest and wails, "What will I tell them? What will I tell Clint and Sherry?"

I look down at her with tears in my eyes. "You tell them that their dad was a good man."

# CHAPTER EIGHTEEN

THE EMPTY METAL CHAIR next to mine accentuates Boone's absence. A vent overhead kicks on and blows heat onto my cold shell of a body.

Stan's eyes, once exuberant and full of life, are forlorn now. I imagine that my eyes resemble his. It's been said that eyes are the window to the soul. If that's truly the case, our souls radiate profound sadness over the group, over everything our eyes touch.

Stan speaks at a slower pace than usual. He offers advice to new attendees as always, but his wisdom comes across with less energy and therefore seems less poignant. If he's anything like me, the loss of Boone haunts him to his core and causes extra bouts of insomnia. The emptiness left behind steals his joy and desire to do much of anything. Simply getting out of bed—to come to group, for instance—saps me of my energy.

"Boone's death is a real trigger for me," I admit during my turn to share. "Every night I struggle with my demons. I know I could easily drive to the casino and gamble away my sorrows... but my promise to Boone keeps me away from the slots."

No one is in a clapping mood today, or any day since his death. I'm not sure this would be the time to clap, but stories of conquering our condition usually prompt mild applause under normal circumstances. This is far from a normal circumstance.

Derrick adjusts his dark hat from his chair. "I'm not going to lie, I relapsed the other night. I couldn't take it. I needed something to take my mind off everything." He glances at Boone's empty chair. "It didn't work," he adds, his eyes shimmering beneath the brim. "Nothing works."

I breathe deeply to hold the tears at bay.

Stan clears his throat. "It makes sense that you'd lean on the race track during trauma, even though you know betting won't help you in the long run," he speaks slowly, his voice slightly strained. "But I can assure you, and everyone here, that as much as this feeling seems permanent, it isn't. It's temporary." His weary eyes scan the group. "We'll get through this."

I catch a newbie in the corner giving a look of bewilderment.

"Boone was my sponsor... and a good man," I speak to the newbie, briefing him. "I wish you could've had the opportunity to meet him so you could understand."

"I feel the same way," says Natalie, her ponytail oddly absent. "Everyone would be better off with a Boone in their life."

———

Tonight, as on most nights as of late, I lie awake in the darkness.

"Slugger..." Boone's voice wafts through my mind, a fleeting memory. I wish I could grab hold of it, contain it somehow, so it could never be forgotten.

"Family ain't always blood... Brother from a different momma..." His thick accent swims through my mind, leaving behind ripples.

I battle the impulse to jump out of bed and run out of this house to escape the feelings. I force myself to remain in bed and feel everything—the gnawing pain and sadness.

I know it's important to feel every ounce of this.

*It's temporary,* I remind myself repeatedly.

———

At the urging of Linda, claiming that I "need to get out of the house and move around a bit," I agree to go on a hike with her.

"It's an hour hike, tops," she says over the phone. "Dress warm. It's a cool day."

I meet her near the base of the mountain wearing my North Face vest. We head toward the color-changing trees—leaves of brown and orange and yellow clinging to the finger-like branches. We step onto the dirt path and proceed up the walkway. Our feet crunch the occasional dead leaf and rotten twig. Voices chatter in the distance, somewhere up above us, reminding us that we aren't alone.

My feet move slowly, weighted down by life's misfortunes. I hear Boone's voice in the wind from all sides of me. I could try to shake it off, but I don't want to. As far as I'm concerned, my brother moves with us on this path. He matches each heavy step that I take. He too hears the approaching stream burbling beyond the thickets of trees.

"Watch your step," Linda says, hopping over a protruding rock.

I jump over the pointy rock, Boone following in my footsteps.

"Look!" Linda points to the cascading water. "How about a quick pit stop?"

"Sure." I imagine Boone and me saying in unison.

We step off the path and push through the woods, our hands brushing away the branches, until we reach the edge of the murmuring stream. A sunbeam touches down on the water, leaving behind gleaming traces of orange and yellow on the moving wrinkles.

Linda sits on a bed of moss. I join her there. Boone retreats into my mind, giving us some space.

"It's beautiful, isn't it?" Linda's eyes follow the water downstream.

"Not as beautiful as you," I say, and our eyes meet.

She grins at me. "You're too kind."

I put my hand on hers, an old habit. Unfazed, she allows it to remain there. The warmth from her hand flows through my palm, up my sleeved arm. I want more, so much more. I lean in for a kiss but she turns her cheek.

She looks down at the moss. "I'm sorry... I can't."

I start to wilt inside like the leaves overhead. "I... uh... I just got lost in the moment," I stammer.

"I don't know what to say." She looks up at me again.

"Still confused?"

"Yeah. About a great many things, unfortunately."

"At least you're honest," I say, but inside I worry that I'm going to be relegated to the friend zone forever.

"I just need more time," she says softly. "More time to sort things out."

Crestfallen, I ask, "How much more time?"

She puts her hand on mine, her eyes planted on me. "Can't hurry love," she says, a tribute to the classic song.

"I can wait for you."

―――――――

I climb up the hill through mounds of leaves, a bouquet of flowers in one hand. I push the creaking cemetery gate open at the top of the hill and step onto the leaf-laden moss. I spot Janice's shaded headstone from afar. I trek through the graveyard, feet crashing against the brittle leaves.

At her headstone, I identify the wilted bouquet I left previously. I remove the old cluster of flowers from its place and replace them with the new flowers. I step back, the cool autumn air rushing over me.

"Hey, Janny... I have so much to tell you, but I don't know where to begin..." My racing thoughts press down on me, paralyzing me for a moment.

I gather my breath, close my eyes. Breathe in and out. I envision her standing before me, my sweet Janny here in the flesh. She beams at me and immediately I don't feel so cold.

I tell her about my job loss, how money is tight these days and I'm barely making ends meet.

I bring up Jay. "I saw him. Well, I guess you already know that. But he's still trying to make a name for himself. He hasn't quit after all these years." My voice starts to wobble. "You should have seen him out there. Our little boy's a man, Janny."

I gather more breath, my body shaking this time. I open my eyes and stare at her headstone. "I lost him all over again, Janny," I say, thinking of his final words and the out of service messages. "I tried this time, I really did. I want him in my life so badly... I don't know what to do... I don't want to force myself on him if he doesn't want me around..." Tears begin to fall. "I've lost so much..." A tear drops onto a leaf.

My thoughts turn to Boone grabbing at his chest, then Boone in the hospital bed. My brother on his deathbed. "You would've loved Boone. He called me slugger." I let out a painful chuckle at the thought. "You'd be proud of me, I guess. I'm finally staying away from the slots... Hard to believe, right? But I'm doing it..."

Then I think of Linda, and our tumultuous relationship, whatever it is now. I think of how my Janny was always there for me. She was never confused or aloof unless I had done something to deserve it. She just wanted me around, to spend more time with her and Jay. Why was that so difficult for me at the time?

"I don't know where to go from here, Janny. What should I do? What can I do about anything? I've been swinging the bat. I've been trying so incredibly hard..."

I pause for a long while, pondering my own words. The cool wind picks up again, blowing through me.

I speak to her headstone, "Can you show me a sign? Can you or God do that for me, wherever you are? I want to believe God's at work but I'd love a sign..."

# CHAPTER NINETEEN

**FROM LINDA'S LIVING ROOM,** through a large window, I intently watch the flurries float down like white confetti from a gray sky. The prospect of a new year gives me hope that better things are to come.

Linda joins me on the couch with a glass of wine for each of us. She passes me a glass of merlot with a tremulous hand. She flips on the TV with her remote, tuning into the daylong New Year's Eve event broadcast from Times Square. Celebrities, some donning festive hats, reminisce over their year. One middle-aged singer waxes poetic about his loving wife. The crowd lets out a well-timed "*aww.*"

Some celebrity teen unknown to me, with spiked blond hair, appears on-screen and shares a cliché statement about time. "Time is so fleeting," he says through a microphone. The anchor nods in agreement, saying, "You're so right," but stops short of calling him a genius. Adoring teen fans scream and cheer in the background at his obvious adage.

"Thanks for inviting me over," I say. I hold up my glass. We clink glasses together. She doesn't say anything. Her attention turns to the TV once again, staring blankly at the screen. She nervously taps the floor with her shoe. Her hand trembles slightly over her glass.

"Are you all right?" I glance at her vibrating hand.

She turns to me. "I... umm... I—"

"What's wrong? You're acting off again?"

"I've been doing a lot of thinking about the future," she says. "A lot of reflecting"

"How so?"

"You know that feeling you get when you're not quite in the right place?"

"More than you know."

"I've been struggling with that." She sets her wine on the glass coffee table near our feet, then leans back on the sofa, hands fidgeting. "I know you've been very patient with me. More than I deserve, I suppose."

I want to nod but I refrain.

"Decisions have been weighing on me for months," she adds. "Decisions that affect everyone in my life including you."

My stomach turns over at the thought. "And what decisions are these?"

"I feel terrible, Jet. You have to believe me when I tell you that I didn't intend to hurt you in any way. You're an amazing guy but—"

"Did you really bring me to your house on New Year's Eve to tell me it's over?"

"This is an in-person talk, not a phone or text talk. I wanted to give you the respect you deserve." She avoids eye contact.

"So *that's* what this is? Here I thought you wanted me over to spend a romantic evening with you on New Year's Eve. I guess I was sorely mistaken." My words burn my throat.

She finally looks into my eyes. "Jet, I received a job offer. It's going to allow me to become president of the Sherman, Texas, division. It's a once-in-a-lifetime opportunity." Her eyes pierce me. "I've been incredibly torn by it, hence my ongoing confusion," she reveals at last. "Obviously it entails my relocation."

"So, you're leaving?" My voice showcases my feelings of betrayal.

"I've decided to accept the position, yes," she says, barely above a whisper.

I'm speechless, utterly speechless.

"I have to take a swing at this, Jet. I can't let it pass me by." Her voice grows louder.

"I guess you don't really *need* me in your life, after all, then. So much for the puzzle piece and all that jazz..."

She sighs deeply. "They wanted my decision by Friday, and you've been going through so much, I didn't want to—"

I wave her off. "No, no, I get it. You didn't think poor little Jet could handle the news, so instead you string me along for months."

The Backwards K     203

She wags her head. "No, I didn't know for sure about any of this. I had to think long and hard about all of it. It was complicated."

"Let me guess, you want to remain friends?"

"We can still see each other—"

"Right." I shake my head vehemently. "*Wow* is all I can say."

She reaches for my hand. I yank my hand away.

She recoils. "I want you to know how proud of you I am. You've been swinging so hard." Her pupils flare. "You've inspired me," she says.

"Happy New Year to me," I say, my voice laced with sarcasm. "This feels like a second breakup, if you want my honest opinion."

"I'm sorry, Jet. Again, I never intended to hurt you."

My breath quickens. I feel like I'm going to hyperventilate.

She places a gentle hand on my shoulder. "I want what's best for you. I didn't want you chasing after me." She lets out a slight whimper. "As much as I hate to admit it, your path is different than mine."

"I guess so!" The words roll off my tongue like fire.

She flinches, pulls her hand away.

I break down, shaking my head, tears flying every which way. "I'm... sorry... it's just... I'll miss you..."

"I already miss you," she says, wrapping her arms around me.

———

At group, I clutch the armrest of my metal chair as an attempt to steady my hand, my emotions. "I'm so angry at her for leaving me," I tell the group. "She knows that I don't do well with loss, but she left anyway. She's so selfish."

Stan interjects, "I know it's hard to hear, and I'm not taking sides, believe me, but remember that she's not responsible for your happiness."

I look up at him. I could take a swipe at his face.

"The most important thing in your life right now is your refraining from gambling. That has to be your primary focus." His words set my blood aflame.

I tighten my grip on the armrest.

———

My foot presses down on the accelerator. The wheels spin through the snow. I nearly lose control of the vehicle at a turn in the road. I stomp again on the pedal, hurtling myself toward the distant building with the blinking lights, the hope of a special winter jackpot.

I swerve into the casino parking lot, a feeling of numbness filling my body. I exit my car as all the times before and proceed to the entrance. I walk through the doorway and stand there for a moment, then another moment, and another. Another.

I eye my lucky slot machine. It doesn't call my name. It just sits there, lights blinking at me like a robot.

I take a single step toward it and Boone's voice bounces through my mind, "You promise me you ain't gonna go relapsin', okay? You just promise."

My desire turns to rage. I stare at the machine fiercely, like I could attack it, tear it apart with my bare hands.

"Sir, would you like some assistance?" A casino worker leans in front of me, looking me over.

I snap out of my daze. "No... no, you can't help me."

He squints at me. "Okay... Sir—"

I turn on a heel, dismissing him. I turn my back to the slot machines, to the bells and flashing lights. I turn my back on the fraudulent excitement and escape from reality. Mostly, I turn my back on my condition, a part of myself that I'm willing to let go.

I advance to the doors. I visualize Boone marching along with me, his chin held up high.

"Atta boy, slugger," he says, his snowy white beard bouncing with each step. "Atta slugger..."

# CHAPTER TWENTY

**TODAY MARKS LINDA'S MOVING DAY.** My heart still stings from Linda's startling decision to leave. Half of me understands—and condones—her decision to take a swing at the opportunity, while the other half burns over it. I've contemplated driving to her house today to offer assistance, but I realize that the plug needs to be pulled if I'm to get over her, if that's even possible. Plus, knowing Linda, I'm sure she's hired a moving company to help.

This decision of hers effectively disassembled that nearly flawless puzzle of us, then she burned the other pieces. She watched with a vacant stare as the puzzle disintegrated into ash. I find this troubling, having to give up on a puzzle so close to completion, but not every aspect of life can reach its full potential. Regrettably, I know this far too well. I'm tired of losing everyone close to me. I guess relationships have never been my forte.

I sit on the edge of my unmade bed and I unlock my cell. I press on my picture app. With a groaning heart, I swipe through the images with a finger—Linda and I dressed up and posing together at a dinner; she and I making funny faces in one of those photo booths; and holding hands before a lighthouse. These were taken before our relationship turned tumultuous, before the powers that be offered her the new job, before she apparently realized that she doesn't truly *need* me in her life. I gravitate to these pictures daily because they serve as proof that the puzzle existed at one time, even if only for a short while.

Then I find myself flipping to my banking app after the thought of the approaching rent due date next month flutters into mind. $825.56 appears on the screen, reminding me of my financial woes. At this rate, I won't be able to stay here much longer. I need to make some decisions of my own. Soon.

The idea of once again trying my hand at the slots enters my mind. I could double my money, triple it perhaps, or lose all of it in one fell swoop. But I made a promise to Boone that I must uphold, and gambling is not a sustainable or honorable living, anyway. I could search for another job, I suppose, but I'm certain my previous employer won't offer a glowing recommendation, so what's the use? I could continue attending the conventions, selling a few collectible items—*it has its moments*—but I can't truly make a living from that side gig.

I visit the refrigerator, not out of a desire to eat, but because I realize that I need to eat something to survive. Not many choices remain in this bare fridge. I place a slice of recently expired ham and cheese in between stale bread. I don't have any mayo, so a dry sandwich will have to do. I force the sandwich down my throat, like a bird choking on a worm.

I leave the apartment, the icy air cutting through me. I drive toward the grocery store and notice the flashing gas light. I turn into a gas station. I pump the gas, my breath roiling from my mouth like smoke. My gloveless hand trembles, sticking to the pump's handle. I pay at the pump with a near-maxed-out credit card. If it isn't a life necessity, I charge it to a card these days. My credit lines are running out.

Teeth chattering, I get in the car. I put on the heat full blast and leave the station. In a moment of weakness, I purposely choose an alternate route to the grocery store, one that intersects with Linda's house. I slowly drive by her lavish home, eyeing the fleet of moving trucks parked out front and men lugging boxes down her walkway. I look for her, her warm smile, but she's not here.

I turn around at the end of the street, and drive back toward her house. I park on the other side of the street, next to a sidewalk, far enough away to be out of the crew's sight. They lumber to the trucks lugging the heavy boxes. I imagine that somewhere inside one of those boxes resides her father's urn and my signed baseball card to go along with it. The thought slices at my chest.

Then, Linda appears without warning in her front doorway, her attention fixed on one of the movers. She points a finger in the direction of the trucks, giving orders. Her face appears stern, devoid of any gentleness. I consider stepping out of the car and approaching her to see if the sight of me softens her expression, but I can't will myself out of the vehicle.

I remind myself of the facts: *I waited for her. I gave her the time she asked for, put up with her confusion and complications, then she ripped me to shreds... on New Year's Eve.*

I camp out in my car for what feels like hours, catching the occasional fleeting glimpse of her. I wonder if she's happy with her decision to leave, if she has any regrets. "I swung," I whisper as she points at another box. "I swung for us and I struck out. Can you say the same?"

She turns her back to the workers, turns her back on me, and re-enters her house. I can't stand to watch any longer. I put my car in gear and speed off, memories of us swirling in my head like a winter storm.

———

On a Saturday afternoon, I reach into the shared mailbox decked with icicles and I discover a brown envelope from former teammate Paul Frankey. I open the letter over the slushy parking lot. It's an invitation to come his way next month to watch some spring training baseball in Fort Myers, Florida, and "talk business."

I ponder the letter, this opportunity like many before it. I glance down at the bottom of the letter, and see his cell number written there. I ponder and ponder and ponder.

Back in the apartment, I don't crumple the letter. I don't throw it away. I set it on the kitchen table and pace around the room, trying to think of a reason not to call. I scan my derelict apartment—the peeling, water-stained walls and ceiling, the ragged couch, the duffle bag perched near the off-track closet door.

*I need to get outta here. I need to choose a different road.* I swing my eyes back to the table, to the unfurled letter. *I need to stop letting this opportunity pass me by. I need to swing. I'm a baseball guy. I've always been a baseball guy. I can't keep running.*

The next morning, I phone Frankey. He doesn't answer, reminding me of Jay.

I swing again at noon; the phone rings six times and then directs me to his voicemail. I don't know what to say in a message, so I end the call.

I swing a third time at three o'clock.

"Paul Frankey speaking."

"Frankey!"

"Is this who I think it is?"

"It's Jet."

"Well, how about that, then?" He chortles. "I was beginning to think you'd forgotten about me."

"How could I forget about the great Paul Frankey?"

He laughs again. "So, what do you say? How about a trip to Florida?"

"I'll tell ya what, I'll join you under two conditions—"

"Sure."

"First, I'll need a place to stay."

"*Check.* You can stay with me."

"Second, tell that boss of yours to send someone with some baseball common sense over to Arizona to pay attention to my boy." I think of Jay standing on a mound in the desert sun, peering in to the catcher for the signs. "He deserves to be seen... *really* seen."

Silence.

I await Frankey's response.

I hear him breathing into the phone.

"Deal," he says. I swear I can hear him smiling over the phone.

He gives me directions to his home, tells me I have a place to stay for as long as I need. "I can't wait. Just like the old days," he says. "So, what's new with you, by the way?"

I'm the one giving a long pause now. "Let's just say... we have a lot of catching up to do."

---

"Welcome to JetBlue Park," says the PA announcer, "and tonight's spring training game between the Red Sox and Yankees."

An applause erupts through the stands. I look out to left field, see a Green Monster wall modeled after *the* Green Monster in Boston. This Monster includes seating within the wall as well as on top of it. Fans lean over the edge of the wall's peak, red umbrellas poking at the darkening blue marble sky behind them. The lights shine over the green-striped field where the players take part in pregame fielding and throwing routines.

Frankey and I sit side-by-side on the first base side of home plate. Frankey pulls a radar gun from his bag, points it out onto the field, testing it while the pitcher throws his warm-up pitches. "They say this kid could be something special if he could develop a third pitch. Skip's working with him on a splitter. We'll see."

The gangly pitcher fires another pitch, this time popping the glove with increased oomph. It clocks in at 88 mph.

I lean over to Frankey. "Impressive for a two-seamer."

A tap on my shoulder spins me around in the seat. "Jet Brine?" I look up to see a man step down the stairs in the aisle to my side. "I knew that was you!" His voice projects his excitement. He eagerly shakes my hand and introduces himself as Newman Hilane. "We're so happy to have you here."

Another man appears behind him and reaches in to shake my hand as well. "Kirk Logan," he says from a stair. "We were all wondering what it would take to get you down here." He nods at Frankey. "This one must have done some coercing, huh?"

I chuckle. "Something like that."

They depart after a few more pleasantries. People occupy the seats around us.

A woman in the seat below me, wearing a nondescript red cap, jots down notes on a clipboard. She glances back at me several times. Frankey notices and nudges me with an elbow. I don't know if he's trying to motivate me into saying something to her, or if he simply wants to make sure I notice her noticing me.

Another scout approaches my side from the aisle, holds out a hand. He announces himself quickly and I don't catch his full name. I nod and smile. "I heard through the grapevine that congratulations are in order," he says.

I cock my head at him. I glance at Frankey's deadpan face, then back at the scout.

"Your son's name came down the pipeline," the scout elaborates.

He must see my baffled expression because he clarifies further. "I trust you heard that the Sox signed Jay to their double-A affiliate in Portland." he says with a slightly rising inflection.

I look to Frankey again. He winks at me and grins.

The scout shrugs. "Well, congrats again, and I'll see you around."

I face Frankey. "When were you gonna tell me?"

"I wanted to surprise you, but I should've known word travels fast." He smiles again. He hands me a scouting brochure of some sort. "Check out page twenty-two."

I flip to the page, spot Jay's name in bold below a half-page image of him delivering a pitch. His schedule spreads over the page beneath his name. I pull out a pen and circle a couple dates on the sheet, plotting my next move, as Frankey watches.

The woman in front of me turns to me as I replace the pen. "Sorry, I couldn't help but over-hear..." She extends her hand. We shake. "You're Jet Brine," she says. "You're Jay Brine's dad..."

I smile at her mention of *dad*, a designation that I've longed to hear.

"Yeah... I'm Jay Brine's dad," I say proudly.

She hands me her card. I study the card carefully, blink twice at it, look up at her as she smiles. I gaze at the card again, her first name, **LINDA**, in all caps staring back at me. The crack of a bat spins her around in her seat. A foul ball. She scribbles down more notes.

Grinning, I lift my eyes to Janice's garden in the sky, feel sweet Janny beaming down on me with her warm smile, reassuring me that I'm in the right place at the right time, that she or God is giving me a sign at last.

A loud applause ripples through the stadium.

I bring my gaze back down to earth. People stand from their seats, the applause mounting. I eye the scoreboard, the 0-2 count glowing red on the green wall.

The batter steps back into the box. He digs his cleats into the dirt. In my mind's eye, I imagine I'm in his place doing the same; I'm the one standing in that box, readying myself for the pitch. The only question is a simple one: if the ball's headed for the strike zone, will I swing or watch it pass me by?

The pitcher comes to a set. He leans in to get the sign, his face contorting.

The cheering rings through my ears, launching me back in time, to the field where my nightmare began.

The pitcher goes through his motions and everything plays out in slow motion. The ball tumbles toward me and I swear I can see every red stitch.

I go to swing...

The bat lifts from my shoulder.

I swing with all my strength. The ball screams off the bat. The crowd noise rises as the ball leaves the park like a lightning bolt. Cameras flash across the stands, blanketing the field with additional light.

I round the bases in a home run trot, my head tilted up at the glowing stars. A star flickers back at me, saying hello, reassuring me that God is at work all around us, and *for* us... if we simply decide to swing the bat.

CPSIA information can be obtained
at www.ICGtesting.com
Printed in the USA
BVOW03s2206231017
498472BV00001B/1/P